John St. Loe Strachey

Cat and Bird Stories from the Spectator

John St. Loe Strachey

Cat and Bird Stories from the Spectator

ISBN/EAN: 9783744746427

Printed in Europe, USA, Canada, Australia, Japan

Cover: Foto ©Andreas Hilbeck / pixelio.de

More available books at **www.hansebooks.com**

CAT AND BIRD STORIES

FROM THE "SPECTATOR."

CAT AND BIRD STORIES

FROM THE "SPECTATOR"

TO WHICH ARE ADDED

*SUNDRY ANECDOTES OF HORSES, DONKEYS, COWS,
APES, BEARS, AND OTHER ANIMALS, AS WELL
AS OF INSECTS AND REPTILES*

WITH AN INTRODUCTION BY

JOHN St. LOE STRACHEY

LONDON

T. FISHER UNWIN

PATERNOSTER SQUARE

1896

CONTENTS.

CONTENTS.

INTRODUCTION.[1]

— ◦◦◦ —

I.

IN a recent volume I collected the Dog Stories that have appeared in the *Spectator*. In the present are to be found *Spectator* Stories of Cats, Birds, and Insects, together with a few anecdotes of other creatures, such as Horses, Donkeys, Cows, and Sheep. As was to be expected, the Dogs take the prize for pure intelligence. The Cats, however, are a very good second. The stories about them have, besides, a certain indefinable charm and thrill of amusement which is most delightful. Be the reason what it may, there undoubtedly attaches to the cat a certain sense of humour which makes her most attractive. It may be when we apply the word to the cat that it has more of the old than the new sense about it, more of the meaning which Jonson used when he wrote "Every Man in his Humour," or which Beaumont and Fletcher intended when they wrote "The Humorous

[1] In this Introduction I have resumed portions of an article on "The Cat as an Unconscious Humorist," which appeared in the *Spectator* of August, 1890.

Lieutenant." The fact remains, however, that the cat, in one sense or the other—or perhaps in both—is a very humorous beast.

II.

Bold and absolute statements of this kind require to be supported.

To speak of the cat as a humorist, in any shape or form, sounds, I admit, something very like a contradiction in terms. There are hundreds of people— and by people are meant, of course, only those who belong to the fraternity of cat-lovers, and are bound by that subtle tie of freemasonry that unites all the adherents of the white, the black, the tortoiseshell, the grey, the mustard, and the tabby—who at first sight will be prepared to maintain that the notion of humour must be altogether dissociated from the cat, and that dignity, degenerating in a few exceptional cases into pomposity on the one hand, or insolence and cynicism on the other, is her special quality, and, indeed, the only one marked enough to deserve particular attention. Though I do not altogether agree with this theory, I am prepared to acknowledge that it is the one ordinarily entertained, and further to admit that up to a certain point there is a good deal to be said for it. Looked at merely from one point of view, cats are all dignity and reserve, and display a *hauteur* of demeanour which marks them off as the aristocrats of the animal world. Their absolute refusal to hurry even under the greatest provocation is alone enough to earn them the right to rank as Nature's nobility. I have seen a tabby with a black muzzle who, for cold, calculated, and yet perfectly well-bred insolence, could have given points to a spiteful duchess whose daughter-in-law "wasn't one of us, you know." The heartless and deliberate rudeness of that cat's behaviour on occasion, had she been a man, would have unquestionably justified shooting at sight. The courtiers in the most slavish palace of the East would have rebelled had they received the treatment she meted out daily to those who waited on her hand and foot. After a devoted admirer had hunted breathless and bare-headed over a large garden, and under a blazing July sun, lest puss should lose her dinner, and had at last brought her into the dining-room in his arms, that cat, instead of showing any gratitude, and instead of running with pleasure to the plate prepared for her, has been known to sit bolt upright at the other end of the room, regarding the whole table with a look of undisguised contempt, her eyes superciliously half-shut, and a tiny speck of red tongue protruding between her teeth. If the thing had not been so exceedingly well done, it would have been simply vulgar. As it was, it amounted to the most exasperating form of genteel brutality imaginable. The company having been at last thoroughly stared out of countenance and put down by this monstrous exhibition of intentional rudeness, the cat in question slowly rose to her feet, and digging her claws well into the carpet, stretched and balanced herself, while yawning at the same time with lazy self-satisfaction. After this she proceeded by the most circuitous route obtainable to the plate put out for her, evidently intending it to be clearly understood that she held its presence under the sideboard to be due in some way or other to her own skill and forethought, and that she in no sense regarded herself as beholden to any other person.

Yet another instance of the freezing and offensive dignity which cats are capable of exhibiting occurs to me. I remember to have seen a distinguished diplomatist, trained to hold his own in the courts of kings, and never at a loss to get out of an embarrassing position, or to meet an act of rudeness by a rapier-thrust of wit, utterly put down by a small black kitten. The diplomatist had been playing with the kitten, but he went too far. Instead of making fun for the kitten, he made fun of her, and this she was quick to see and to resent. Determined to mark her sense of his conduct, she at once put a stop to the game, and calmly but resolutely placed her small person in front of the man of ceremony, wrapped her tail neatly round her toes, and gazed at him with an air of pitying contempt. It was an electric moment, and the rest of the company watched with palpitating eagerness the struggle for ascendency. It proved, however, an unequal contest. After a few moments of a regard which told more of sorrow than of anger, the kitten deliberately began to wash her little black face, stopping every now and then, paw in air, to give a look of faint surprise, mingled with disgust, at her antagonist. The situation speedily became ridiculous, but not for the kitten, and in a very short time the diplomatist had evidently admitted himself beaten. The kitten then rose, walked to the window, and placidly gazed out at the landscape, every curve in her back showing her sense of the bad taste which had characterised the incident that had just terminated.

But though the cat is a very dignified animal, and indeed compares favourably with man in that respect, she is often the unconscious cause of humorous situations, owing in a great measure to her unbounded egotism. If a cat is watched carefully in the ordinary relations of domestic life, a thousand instances will be noticed in which the results of her action are exceedingly humorous. Even granted that the cat has herself little or no primary sense of humour, she is capable, when properly understood, of affording intense amusement to others. To realise this fact is a great source of pleasure—nay, of security. It is, indeed, hardly too much to say that unless some means are discovered for taking her down a peg or two every now and then, a cat is an impossible beast to live with. Her pomposity, her formality, and her *de haut en bas* manner of looking at the world, would be unbearable unless we knew how on occasion to turn the laugh against her. Only by enjoying an occasional score off "the furred serpent" can the balance be redressed, and a comfortable *modus vivendi* between man and cat be arranged. Every cat-owner must recall incidents in his experience which in a moment have made up for the many humiliations suffered at the hands of his cat—humiliations received as he stood patiently while puss made an aggravatingly complete periplus of the room before she would deign to walk out of a door, specially opened at her request; or as he fumed on the front doorstep, on a raw November night, trying to induce the priestess of the hearthrug to enter her abode, at his and not her own good time and pleasure.

So much for the cat as a cause of humour, when seen from the man's point of view. We must not forget, however, that there is yet another side to the question—one which has been put with great force and point by Montaigne. "When," says he, "my cat and I entertain each other with mutual apish tricks, as playing with a garter, who knows but that I make my cat more sport than she makes me? Shall I conclude her to be a simple [*i.e.*, a fool], that has her time to begin or refuse to play as freely as I myself have? Nay, who knows but that it is a defect of my not understanding her language (for doubtless cats talk and reason with one another) that we agree no better? And who knows but that she pities me for being no wiser than to play with her, and laughs and censures my folly for making sport for her, when we two play together." Perhaps, too, it is the cat that has the best of the laugh, even when we dub her an unconscious humorist. It would be just like her "subtlety" to be all the while laughing in her sleeve of fur.

Anyhow, in one way or another, the cat is a source of humour. She either makes fun of you, or else gives you the sense of fun. That will, I believe, be admitted on consideration by all cat-lovers, though not perhaps till some great man of letters has arisen and written "Every Cat in her Humour" will the secret of this humorous fascination be laid bare.

III.

Of the bird and other stories in the present volume little need be said except that they have a distinct scientific as well as a literary value. They are not merely good reading, but the record of important facts in Natural History. I will only repeat here what I said in my Introduction to the Dog Stories as to the impossibility of asking all the writers whether they had any objection to the stories reappearing in print. Their original communication of the stories is clearly conclusive evidence that they would have said "Yes," could they have been consulted.

CATS.

———— o•o ————

AN AUTHENTIC ANECDOTE OF AN AUTOMATON.

SIR,—Some time ago, a machine of the cat species was received into our house under distressing circumstances, and adopted by our household. We have all rendered ourselves ridiculous in scientific eyes by becoming much attached to this rescued foundling, and he has assumed, under the name of Bruin, a position of importance which becomes his size, intelligence, and estimate of his own merits. Under the second of these heads, I could furnish you with several interesting particulars; I content myself, however, with one, which relates to our machine of the cat species, and to another machine called a gas-stove. We had one of the latter articles put up in a study beyond the dining-room at the beginning of winter, and Bruin speedily selected it as his own particular fireplace, in preference to the dining-room grate, no doubt because it was less frequented and the heat was more uniform. When the severe cold set in, it

2

struck Bruin's master that it would be comfortable
for him to have the stove to sleep by, and might tend
to modify his erratic habits.   Accordingly the stove
was left alight (at half-strength), and Bruin signified
his approbation by curling himself up in front of it
early in the evening, and sleeping soundly until he
was roused, under protest, and yawning widely, to
a late breakfast, during all the nights and mornings
which have since elapsed.   On Thursday night—
Christmas Eve—his master left home, and it occurred
to me to test Bruin's intelligence concerning that
event.   I left the stove unlighted, and watched his
proceedings when the hour at which he usually retires
to rest arrived.   He marched into the room with the
air of important business to be immediately attended
to which strongly characterises him, looked at the
blank coppery space, uttered an angry cry, and ran
out of the room to the coat-and-umbrella stand in the
hall.   He sniffed at a couple of waterproofs and an
interloping *en tout cas*, but detected the absence of
the familiar great-coat and the sturdy umbrella which
he associates with his master.   Then he rushed upstairs, evidently with a strong sense of injury upon
him, and I followed, to find him crying at the door
of his master's bedroom, which I opened for him.
He jumped on the bed, sniffed about the pillow,
jumped down again, once more cried angrily, and
ran downstairs.   I followed, and took my seat in the
dining-room, pretending not to notice him.   He sat
for two or three minutes in front of the stove, then
came into the dining-room and put his paws upon

my knees, and gazed into my face with a gasp—not a cry, but a mode of speech which this machine has made us understand. I pretended to be puzzled ; he scratched my gown and gasped again. "You are not thirsty, Bruin," I remarked ; "what do you want? I am to get up, am. I, and you will show me?" I suited the action to the word, and he preceded me into the study, stepped inside the fender, put up his paws on the front of the stove, and turned his head towards me over his shoulder with a look of content that I had been clever enough to interpret his meaning, which gave me very sincere satisfaction. As I know that you, Sir, are an advocate for the study of animals otherwise than by the torture of them, I venture to send you this anecdote of an automaton who really seems, to my ignorant mind, to have something like what we fancy we mean by "consciousness."—I am, Sir, &c.,

A CONSTANT READER AND DISCIPLE.

January 2, 1875.

ANOTHER AUTOMATON.

Sir,—I hope you will consider as worthy of record an habitual action on the part of our "conscious automaton" of the cat species, which certainly exhibits a well-connected train of thought.

In this old house there is a staircase with a borrowed light, admitted at a considerable height from the ground, through a balustrade, beneath which there hangs a bell. When our "automaton" finds himself on this staircase—without practicable egress—the door being shut, he leans forward through the balustrade, and literally "touches the bell." Of course, this summons always results in his release by one of his surrounding admirers.—I am, Sir, &c.,

C. T.

January 16, 1875.

A CAT IN LOVE.

SIR,—Your interesting article on Cats in last week's issue prompts me to send you the following entertaining instance of affection between a "domestic Sphinx" and its natural enemy, the dog. The cat in question, which hails from the Isle of Man, is apparently to all intents and purposes *in love* with a fox-terrier inhabiting the same house, and the "spooning" that goes on between them is comic in the extreme. On one occasion, in my presence, the dog (who was seated on a lady's lap) feeling dissatisfied or aggrieved at something or other that was taking place, vented his feelings in a long, low whine or howl. The cat, who was on the hearthrug, turned her head, and gazed with a wistful, sympathetic expression at her suffering friend for some seconds; at last, unable to listen to his weeping any longer, she sprang upon the lady's knees, put her paws round the dog's neck, and kissed his cheek with her lips. This occurred twice, the second time the dog responding to her caresses by licking her back, in the tenderest manner conceivable.

I am not aware whether the exhibition of emotion

or of reason is the less compatible with the automatic theory of animals ; in either case, however, I think the fact I have described is not wholly unworthy the attention of those who have, before now, defended that doctrine in your correspondence columns.—I am, Sir, &c.,   FREDERIC H. BALFOUR.

April 6, 1878.

THE TRAVELLING CAT.

SIR,—During six weeks which I spent at the Diablerets, in Switzerland, several years ago, I had the pleasure of making acquaintance with a very remarkable cat. His mistress, a very clever and interesting lady, nearly related to a celebrated Independent divine, brought him with her to the hotel, and opened his basket in her room. This done, puss looked about him, reconnoitred the locality, and then walked out leisurely, to spend his day in the adjacent fields and woods, returning at night to his bed and supper in his mistress's room. Miss "L." assured me that she had carried the cat all over the Continent with her, and that this was his invariable practice. Perhaps if this letter should fall under her notice, she will favour us with further details respecting her intelligent *compagnon de voyage*. Histories of exceptionally clever and affectionate animals, like the delightful one of "Martin" in your last issue, are of special value, if they cause us to recognise the neglected truth that both the moral and the intellectual qualities of the higher animals vary in individuals between the poles of something like heroism and baseness, genius and idiocy. It is as absurd to talk of "*the* cat" or "*the* dog" being this or that, as of "*the* man" being so. Why do we not take more care to keep up the breeds of the more gifted brutes, and let the foolish and ill-grained ones perish? Is it because our dog-shows and cat-shows make much of some trifle of external form or colour, and totally disregard (except in the case of the sheep-dog trials) all the qualities of the creatures' minds and hearts?—I am, Sir, &c., PHILOZOOIST.

August 27, 1881.

A MUSICAL TOM.

SIR,—Let me add a couple of biographical notes, for the benefit of cat-lovers. I knew a cat, many years ago—a black Tom—rather heavy and dull in his ways, for the most part, but with two qualities very strongly marked—love for music and affectionateness. He knew good music from bad, perfectly well, would sit on the step of a piano with great content and purring, so long as a capable performer was playing, and if the execution were very good indeed, would testify his delight by arching his tail, walking across the keys, and sitting down in the performer's lap. On the other hand, bad playing always drove him away ; and I remember there was one member of the family whose performance always sent him off in disgust. So much for the artistic side of his temperament. Now for the affections. His mother was always very fond of her kittens, and used to sit over them very closely during the first early weeks of their lives,—too closely, her son thought, after he grew old enough to consider about things. So I have more than once seen him go up to her, as she nestled over the young ones in the basket, and apparently whisper something ; whereupon she would get out, stretch herself, and go into the garden for a little fresh air, while he got into her place, and lay over the kittens to keep them warm till she came back, when he resigned his charge to her again. I regret to say that he died, still a comparatively young cat, of distemper. —I am, Sir, &c., RICHARD F. LITTLEDALE.

September 3, 1881.

THE CAT IN THE HOSPITAL.

SIR,—To my regret, my *Spectator* of the 20th did not reach my hand until the 24th. I was deeply interested in the relation of " Martin's " affection for the persons of the household, and not so much for the house. It happened that on the previous day, the 23rd, I had become acquainted with some facts concerning a fine cat, " Tabby," which do not point in the direction of " Martin's " conduct. In the city of —— (never mind where), there is a large hospital of wooden erections, pavilions. These are being re-placed by permanent structures. To allow of these being erected, the occupiers of one ward had to re-move to the other end of the place, to a ward pre-cisely similar, and in every respect as comfortable as the one they left. " Tabby," from its birth, had been a cherished inmate of the old ward, and had gone in and out as a kind of privileged mistress for four or five years, and had been an object of constant atten-tion and affection from both nurses, especially from the younger woman of the two, which affection was duly and well returned by " Tabby." But on the removal of the nurses to the other ward, " Tabby " refused to go with them. She allowed herself to be carried over, but, to the chagrin and mortification of her friends, she returned to her old abode. On hearing these facts, I went over and saw her "hanging about" her old dwelling. My friends, the nurses, hope in time to overcome "Tabby's" strange prejudice. This incident of feline experiences is set down without "note or comment," to be placed alongside of "Martin's" history.—I am, Sir, &c.,

E. H.

September 3, 1881

A DISCIPLINARIAN CAT.

SIR,—The *Spectator* delights in cat stories. May I add one to the interesting list which has from time to time appeared in your columns? Picture to yourself a little girl, about two years of age, sitting on a low stool before a drawing-room fire. Coiled up on the rug is a favourite domestic cat. The child is in a fretful mood, and has been crying for some time. The cat endures the annoyance for some time, though evidently displeased. But even feline patience has its limits. So pussy uncoiled herself, walked up to the child, and gave her a box on the ear with her closed paw, and then lay down again before the fire. The child, taken completely aback, cried louder than ever. Again pussy tried to endure it. Again her patience became exhausted, and she delivered a second box upon the ear, which nearly knocked the child off her stool. It was now the little girl's turn to be enraged. She rushed at the cat, and dragged it round the room by the tail. The story rests on the authority of the child's mother, who was witness of the scene.—I am, Sir, &c.,   M.

January 21, 1882.

ABOUT "DOT."

SIR,—As I am a constant reader of the *Spectator*, I know you take a great interest in domestic animals, and I have long wished to tell you about "Dot." She was handsome as to size ; her coat was a beautiful, glossy black, and at the throat was a pretty, white star. Each day, as the different articles were brought in for dinner and placed on the table, the charge always was, "Now, 'Dot,' come here and take care of this till I come back." "Dot" mounted guard at once, on a chair at the side of the table, and was never known to leave her post till the viands were claimed. Whether it was beef, mutton, fish, or game, all was perfectly safe ; and she was quite contented when a cooked morsel after dinner was given to her as a reward. Her own dinner, though placed close beside her, she never touched, but always waited till it was given to her, however hungry she was known to be.

She was obedient to all orders, one of which was that she was not to come to my room. (I prefer to keep at a respectful distance from even domestic pets, however excellent their individual characters.) But one very cold evening of a very severe winter, " Dot," passing all the other rooms, to which she had perfect freedom, came to my door, and, with a special petition, to which my attention was drawn, as being something quite unusual in cat-language, waited till she was told she might come in. The good creature placed herself before the bright fire, and purred, to her and our great pleasure—a self-invited and truly happy guest. She never once encroached on this one little special favour. Could even the illustrious "Jack" have excelled her when food was the charge?—I am, Sir, &c., M. D.

January, 21, 1882.

A CLEVER CAT.

SIR,—The following proofs of intelligence in a cat you may deem worthy of a space in your columns :— A literary friend of mine at Bath had been often vastly amused at the interest with which her cat appeared to view her proceedings at the writing-table. He would sometimes jump up beside her, and lay his paw on her wrist. On one occasion, however, he leapt on the table in front of her, and watched her narrowly, and with such a preternaturally knowing glance in his bright eye, with his head held slightly on one side, that she was impelled to lay down her pen and look at him. What was her surprise and delight to see him walk deliberately to the inkstand, take a pen in his mouth, and leaping to the floor, commence tracing characters with it on the carpet, fortunately for which, poor Timothy had forgotten the ink ! Another day his mistress said to him in fun, " Oh, Timothy, I have lost a button off my dress ; I wish you would find it ! " The animal looked at her, walked out of the room, and returned in a few minutes with the missing button in his mouth ! Alas ! poor Timothy ! he has disappeared, and this is probably the only permanent record of his winning ways.—I am, Sir, &c., 　　　C. W.

September 2, 1882.

FELINE MOURNERS.

SIR,—Knowing your regard for animals—even for
the despised cat—I send you two cognate anecdotes,
and ask you or your' readers if they can throw any
light on the matter of the expression of grief by
animals. I had a favourite Angora cat, who died
after a week of suffering, the result of an accident.
During his illness, his mother, a fine old cat of the
ordinary sort, was often with him ; but she was not
present at the time of his death. He died late in the
evening, and was taken into the cellar, to await his
burial the next day. When he was brought up, stiff
and cold, in a box, his mother was taken to see him ;
she gave one look, uttered a shriek, and ran away.

On relating this circumstance to a lady, she told
me that there was a pet cat in her family, who was
very fond of this lady's mother. When the latter
was in her last illness, the cat was continually with
her, lying on the bed. The lady died, and the cat
was, of course, not again admitted to the room,
though presenting herself again and again at the
door. When the coffin was being carried downstairs, the cat happened to appear, and, on seeing

3

it, uttered a shriek.   In both these cases, the sound
made was entirely unlike those made by cats under
any circumstances, unless it be the cry made when
in sudden pain.   In the latter case, the most remarkable part remains to be told.   The cat went to
the funeral, and then disappeared for many days.
But after that, she repeatedly attended funerals in
the same cemetery, walking before the clergyman,
her master.—I am, Sir, &c.,

A LOVER OF THE DESPISED.

September 1, 1883.

"TIBS."

SIR,—I am a very little girl, but I wish to tell you a story. A short time ago we lived upon the shores of the Lake Lupioma (Clear Lake), which is one of the most beautiful lakes in California, and there I had a little cat, named "Tibs." There was no regular road to our house on the shore, but only a horse-trail through the bush, and "Tibs" had never passed this way in her life, and all communication was by means of boat and steamers. When we removed from our home we came away in a boat, and after landing two miles further down got directly into a waggon, and rode seven miles up into the forest, where we now live. We left poor "Tibey" behind, knowing she could get her own living very well, and meaning by and by to have her brought to us. Between the place where we now live and the shores of the lake there are two or three small farms, and all around them is forest. But there are innumerable roads, stretching away in every direction. These roads are made by the ox-teams of the wood-choppers; they are very dark and lonely, leading up the mountain-top and into the thickest parts of the pine forest, and then suddenly ending. If you follow one of these, it will lead you many miles away, and then you will come to a spot where some enormous trees have been cut down and been dragged away by the oxen, and all beyond is the dark wood again.

Of course, I was very unhappy about my little friend, but we were all so busy that nobody had time to go and look after her. And so five weeks passed away. One evening, as we were sitting down to supper under a beautiful tall pine tree, we heard a faint mieu, and looking, saw our faithful little cat springing across the stream. We took her into our laps and nursed her all the evening. Will you please tell me in the *Spectator* how "Tibs" found the way?—I remain, your friend,   AGNES.

March 1, 1884.

[We have not the least guess. Perhaps Mr. Romanes would offer a suggestion.—ED. *Spectator.*]

A KITTY GREY.

SIR,—About two months ago, while staying in the Rocky Mountains in Northern Colorado, I witnessed an example of fatherly affection in a tom-cat, which I feel sure you will be interested to hear of. This cat had adopted two motherless kittens; he slept with them at night, guarded them in the daytime, and always superintended their meals, in which latter he showed great unselfishness. For the hostess of the ranche was in the habit of feeding the kittens out of a small bowl of milk laid on the floor, into which they at once would plunge their heads; meanwhile "Kitty Grey," the old tom-cat— quite aware that there was not room for his own great head in it, too—would sit by, complacently watching them, nor move till they had finished, except when his hunger was *very* keen, and then he would dip his paw in now and again and lick it. This was the case when I saw him; and I shall not readily forget the sight of that large grey-and-white cat walking demurely round the bowl to see where he could best insert his paw without disturbing the kittens, and then, with his head much on one side, dipping it delicately in and out, until they had quite finished, when he at once fell-to and drank · up the remainder.—I am, Sir, &c.,   L. C. P.

February 7, 1885.

HOW TOPSY OPENED THE BACK DOOR.

SIR,—The domestic cat is a wonderful animal ; but I fancy your readers are not aware that they can open doors. I have one that always opens the back door himself. His method is simple : he springs up and puts one paw on the latch, the weight causing it to rise, when " Topsy " walks in. I would not believe it for a long time, but now I can account for many missing articles.—I am, Sir, &c., R. S. T.

May 30, 1885.

A WARM-HEARTED CAT.

SIR,—In the extract that you quote from Sir J. Lubbock's Walsall lecture, he says that a certain wasp "knows whether the egg will produce a male or female grub, and apportions the food accordingly." . . . "Does she count?" he asks. Is it an absurd suggestion that the size of the cell and the amount of food supplied may determine the sex of the grub, and that all that the mother does is instinctively to fill the cell, regardless and ignorant of all consequences? The case of the honey-bee is somewhat analogous; for if not sex, at least mature development, depends on conditions of food and cell; the worker-grub, properly fed and celled, can, as is well known, become a queen.

I can parallel your example of animal sympathy. I had a cat who carried to an old bitch who had partly suckled him, dainties to tempt her appetite in her last illness. But *his* feelings were more enduring. After the poor old dog had been removed by poison, the cat would not for some time go near myself or the gardener, though previously much attached to both; evidently he thought we were implicated in the removal of his foster-mother.—I am, Sir, &c.,

FRATER.

February 19, 1887.

SYMPATHY IN CATS AND DOGS.

SIR,—I know you have a high opinion of the dog's character, but of the "harmless, necessary cat" perhaps you may not think so well as he or she deserves. The following anecdote of my own "Black Beauty," or "Professor Blackie," as I often call him, may find a place in your generous paper.

A favourite Pomeranian dog was cruelly blinded by a carter's lash, and, while his owner tenderly bathed the inflamed eyes, "Blackie," the sleek tom-cat, always sat by with a kindly look of pity in his luminous green eye. When "Laddie," the blind dog, was called in at night, he often failed to find the door, or would strike his venerable head against the posts. "Blackie," having noted this difficulty, would jump off his warm cushion by the kitchen fire, trot out with a "mew" into the dark night, and in a few minutes return with "Laddie" shoulder-to-shoulder, as it were, and the friends would then separate for the night. "Laddie," when younger, had quietly resented the attentions shown by his owner to a fascinating kitten, who used to frolic with his long, fringed tail; but he was too noble to show active dislike. When the kitten died in convulsions—a victim to nerves and a ball of cotton—and its owner bent over the stiffened form in grief, "Laddie" came gravely up and kissed it. He followed to the grave, and for many days was seen by his mistress to go up the garden and sit upon the sod. Was this his way of showing remorse for his former coldness, or might it be an expression of sympathy for his bereaved owner?—I am, Sir, &c.,

AN OLD READER.

August 20, 1887.

CATS AS HUMORISTS.

SIR,—After reading your article on " Cats as Humorists," I am obliged to send you an anecdote of mine, a long-haired, black Persian.   Living in the suburbs, we are infested by cats of all kinds, and are perpetually driving them away, aided by the said long-haired favourite, who pursues them off the premises with hair and tail standing wildly erect, and presenting a most alarming appearance.   We feel that this violent demonstration must be a joke, as the same cat constantly carries the remains of her own dinner about twenty-five yards, across an open space and up some steps, to feed the identical animals she has driven off an hour or two previously.—I am, Sir, &c.,

A. E. L.

August 16, 1890.

A CAT AND A HEDGEHOG.

Sir,—Have you space for one more cat-story? Many years ago I was living in a house where a hedgehog was kept for the destruction of blackbeetles. I had heard that hedgehogs would eat mice; and one day finding the cat playing with a mouse she had caught, I took it from her and gave it to the hedgehog, who immediately proceeded to devour it. The cat was at first furious, and began to claw at the hedgehog, who, however, only elevated its spines, and quietly went on with its meal, and the cat soon desisted from the attempt to recover her lost prey.

The curious part of the story is what followed. For weeks afterwards, whenever the cat caught a mouse, she went in search of the hedgehog, and did not rest until she found it, and had placed the mouse where the hedgehog could secure it. I cannot say how often this was done, but am sure it was not fewer than half-a-dozen times. Perhaps some of your readers may be able to define the motive which induced these repeated acts of self-denial.—I am, Sir, &c., JOSHUA SING.

August 30, 1890.

CATS' INTELLIGENCE.

SIR,—My mother used to tell a story of an old cat who used to sit on the table beside her mother's old housekeeper, and play with her cotton-balls (reels were not in those days). It was a common custom to stick pins or needles in these cotton-balls if a pincushion was not at hand. This cat, finding herself pricked by the needles when playing with these balls, used to draw them out first with her teeth in order to play with comfort. If people would treat cats as they do dogs, and study them as much, they would be repaid by the amount of intelligence and sagacity shown.—I am, Sir, &c.,   SALF.

February 7, 1891.

A NEW FOSTER-MOTHER FOR KITTENS.

SIR,—The letter signed " F. Simcox Lea," which appeared in the *Spectator* of May 27th, induces me to give you an account of a similar incident at my residence in Surrey, differing in our case only inasmuch as it has been a recurring one for at least six consecutive years. The birds (which we call " bluetits ") for the first two years built under an inverted flower-pot on a ground-floor window-sill, but the pot being transferred to another position, they followed it there. We have often looked at them when sitting, and the bird has frequently remained on the nest while the pot was lifted and replaced. Once the greater part of the half-fledged brood fluttered off, and got scattered about, and had to be replaced through the hole in the top, seeming none the worse. Once away, they do not seem to return to the nest, as do the broods of the kind of wren which builds a round ball of a nest in the bushes. I unintentionally put the whole dozen or so of young birds out of one of these nests one Sunday morning, under a fierce fire of scolding from the old bird, found them all there again the following Sunday, and (finally, I imagine) put them all out again on the Sunday after that.

It may interest your readers who care about this sort of subject, to hear of the singular incident at our farm two years ago, of a hen taking charge of three kittens. The mother-cat must have taken them herself an hour or two after their birth and placed them under the hen, which had made a nest for herself two or three yards off under the manger in a cowshed. I saw the cat and her progeny lying on the straw directly after their birth, and noticed the hen on her nest. Returning an hour or two later, the cowman showed me the kittens under the hen, wondering how they had got there, as nobody else had been in the shed, and he had not touched them. Till the kittens grew too big, the hen never left them ; the cat used to go away foraging, and come down every now and then, throw herself down alongside the hen and nurse her young ones, sometimes lying with her head under, and her paws almost round, the hen's neck. As the kittens got older, it was droll to see their foster-mother following them about and trying to cover them with her wings. For some six weeks it was quite the sight of the neighbourhood. I suppose incidents of the sort are not very unfrequent, though rare to one's own personal knowledge.—I am, Sir, &c.,

June 3, 1893.

ANOTHER FOSTER-MOTHER FOR KITTENS.

SIR,—A somewhat similar incident to that recorded by Mr. Egerton in the *Spectator* of June 3rd took place some years back at Northrepps Hall, near Cromer, the seat of the late Sir Fowell Buxton. A large colony of parrots and macaws had been established there, for whom a home had been provided near the house in a large open aviary, with hutches for them to lay in. But the birds as a rule preferred the woods, at any rate during the summer, only coming home at feeding-time, when, on the well-known tinkling of the spoon on the tin containing their food, a large covey of gaily plumaged birds came fluttering down to the feeding-place, presenting a sight not often to be seen in England. The hutches being then practically deserted, a cat found one of them a convenient place to kitten in. While the mother-cat was away foraging, one of the female parrots paid a chance visit to the place, and finding the young kittens in her nest, at once adopted them as her own, and was found by Lady Buxton's man covering her strange adopted children with her wings. Whether this practice was continued, as in Mr. Egerton's case, or only adopted on this one occasion, I cannot say.

May I be permitted to add another count to the indictment against the "odious" and "odorous" black-beetle or "cockroach," formulated in your amusing article on "Household Pests"? The wretched creature is very fond of the paste with which in former days (one seldom sees them now) the paper titles of books were affixed to their backs. When living on the Undercliff of the Isle of Wight, my house swarmed with these foul insects. They drowned themselves in one's milk, swam in one's soup, and nibbled one's pastry. They even invaded our beds ; nor was it conducive to a night's calm repose, on turning down the bedclothes, to see one or more of these wretches scurrying away over the sheets. We laid traps for them—a very clever dodge —by filling soup-plates with beer, with a fringe of split sticks resting on the ground, by which they might climb, and after having drunk their fill, lose their heads, tumble in and be drowned. The abundance of these pests may be gathered when I say that one morning we found between twenty and thirty of various ages, sizes, and colours drowned in the beer in our own bedroom. My study having the kitchen fireplace behind it, was a favourite resort for these horrible insects. On the shelves by the fireplace there were a number of volumes with the white paper labels I have spoken of. These labels, to my annoyance, I found gradually disappearing ; not peeling off, but wasting away in comminuted fragments. For some time this was a mystery to me ; at last, while I sat writing late at the other side of the room, I was conscious of slight rustlings and scrapings by the fireplace, and on examining my bookshelves I found the cockroaches making their supper on the backs of my books.

Subsequent alterations in the house removed the kitchen, and the loss of the warmth which cock-roaches so much delight in made them shift their quarters, and the injury to my library ceased ; and the kitchen being in a remote part of the house, their visits to the bedrooms became less frequent. Like the writer of the article, I tried a hedgehog. The worthy animal did his best. He devoured cock-roaches to repletion, an over-full meal sometimes making him almost a greater nuisance than the in-sects themselves. But what could one do among so many ? He died at last, I believe, from over-devotion to his task, and his praiseworthy but ineffectual attempts to rid us of the pest came to an end. Not so the pest itself, and but for the structural alterations I have mentioned, and carefully stopping all the crannies in which the cockroaches nestled by the fireplace, it would have been as great as ever.

EUMUNT VENABLES.

A CAT AND HER KITTENS.

SIR,—I have often read with interest your stories of animals. Perhaps the following may find favour with your cat-loving readers :—We have two cats—the mother, Betsy, and her daughter Lina, two years old. When the kittens came, we had always kept one of each family, but we decided that the next that came should all be destroyed. Accordingly, when Lina's four kittens arrived, they were all drowned. Three days later, Betsy had six kittens. On the cellar being opened in the morning where their bed was, Lina immediately took up the six kittens one by one to the attic, a distance of seventy stairs, doing it as quickly as possible, the last twelve being so steep that she had to hold her head very high to prevent her knocking the kitten she held in her mouth. Having deposited them all in a box, she tried to take the mother too to the supposed place of safety. After four were drowned, she repeated this with the remaining two several times, nursing them as though they were her own in the box, not allowing the mother to keep them downstairs at all. By what method of reasoning did she arrive at the intended destiny of these kittens? or did she think they were her own given back to her? —I am, Sir, &c.,   F. B.

July 14, 1894.

THE STORY OF THE BEAUTIFUL PERSIAN.

SIR,—As the dogs are having a good time in the *Spectator*, I hope you will allow the cats a share. Your readers may be interested in hearing of the crafty trick of a black Persian. "Prin" is a magnificent animal, but withal a most dainty one, showing distinct disapproval of any meat not cooked in the especial way he likes—viz., roast. The cook, of whom he is very fond, determined to break this bad habit. Stewed or boiled meat was accordingly put ready for him, but, as he had often done before, he turned from it with disgust. However, this time no fish or roast was substituted. For three days that saucer of meat was untouched, and no other food given. But on the fourth morning the cook was much rejoiced at finding the saucer empty. "Prin" ran to meet her, and the good woman told her mistress how extra affectionate that repentant cat was that morning. He did enjoy his dinner of roast that day (no doubt served with a double amount of gravy). It was not till the pot-board under the dresser was cleaned on Saturday that his artfulness was brought to light.   There, in one of the stewpans, at the back behind the others, was the contents of the saucer of stewed meat.   There was no other animal about the place, and the other two servants were as much astonished as the cook at the clever trick played on them by this terribly spoilt pet of the house.   But cook was mortified at the thought of that saucer of roast beef.   I know this story to be true, and I have known the cat for the last nine or ten years.   It lives at Clapham.—I am, Sir, &c.,　　　　　　　A. Z.

February 16, 1895.

A CAT-AND-DOG FRIENDSHIP.

SIR,—The interesting letter, " A Canine Nurse," in the *Spectator* of May 18th, recalls to mind an equally curious event in cat and dog life which occurred some years since in a house where I was living, but with the additional interest of a hen being also implicated.

In the back-kitchen premises of an old manor-house, amongst hampers, and such like odds and ends, a cat had a litter of kittens. They were all removed but one, and as the mother was frequently absent, a hen began laying in a hamper close by. For a time all things went well, the hen sitting on her eggs and the cat nursing the kitten within a few inches of each other. The brood were hatched out, and almost at the same time the old cat disappeared. The chickens were allowed to run about on the floor for sake of the warmth from a neighbouring chimney, and the kitten was fed with a saucer of milk, &c., in the same place, both feeding together frequently out of the same dish. The hen used to try to induce the kitten to eat meal like the chicks, calling to it and depositing pieces under its nose in the most amusing way, finally doing all in its power to induce the kitten to come, like her chicks, under her wings. The result was nothing but a series of squalls from the kitten, which led to its being promoted from the back to the front kitchen, where it was reared until it was grown up. At this time a young terrier was introduced into the circle, and after many back-risings and bad language on pussy's part, they settled down amicably and romped about the floor in fine style. Eventually the terrier became an inveterate rabbit-poacher—killing young rabbits and bringing them home—a proceeding to which the cat gave an intelligent curiosity, then a passive and purring approval, and finally, her own instincts having asserted themselves, she went off with the dog hunting in the woods. Our own keeper reported them as getting "simply owdacious," being found a great distance from the house ; and keepers of adjacent places also said the pair were constantly seen hunting hedgerows on their beats. On one occasion I saw them myself hunting a short hedge down systematically, the dog on one side, the cat on the other ; and on coming near an open gateway, a hare was put out of her form, and bounding through the open gate was soon off; the dog followed, till he came through the gateway, where he stood looking after the hare ; and the cat joining him, they apparently decided it was too big or too fast to be successfully chased, so resumed the hedge-hunting, each taking its own side as before.

They frequently returned home covered with mud, and pussy's claws with fur, and would lie together in front of the fire, the cat often grooming down the dog, licking him and rubbing him dry, and the dog getting up and turning over the ungroomed side to be finished. This curious friendship went on for six months or more, till the dog had to be kept in durance vile to save him from traps and destruction —the cat, nothing daunted, going on with her poaching, until one day she met her fate in a trap, and so brought her course to an end. The dog was a well-bred fox-terrier, and the cat a tabby of nothing beyond ordinary characteristics, save in her early life having been fostered by a hen, and in her prime the staunch friend and comrade of poor old "Foxie," the terrier. If there are "happy hunting-grounds" for the animals hereafter, and such things are allowed in them, no doubt they will renew their intimacy, if not their poaching forays, together there.—I am, Sir, &c. R. J. GRAHAM SIMMONDS.

June 8, 1895.

AN APOLOGY FOR THE CAT.

SIR,—It seems to me that the great independence of mind shown by even the most domesticated of cats is evidence of a strength of character quite unusual among animals. Of all pets, they give the least trouble; they forage for themselves largely, wash themselves, take exercise of their own accord; less dependent on man than a dog, they are yet capable of strong attachments. My cat, a Persian, is warmly attached to me; even if asleep on any one else's lap, the moment I speak or call her, she runs to me. Whenever she catches a mouse or finds herself some dainty, it is at once brought to me and laid at my feet with a special cry—never used at any other time. When I was ill in the winter and confined to bed for some weeks, pussy was with me day and night, only leaving me for half an hour at dinner-time. Efforts were made to coax her into other rooms equally warm and comfortable, for other invalids were in the house, but nothing would induce her to leave me; and when at last I went abroad for some weeks, I returned to find the poor cat at death's door. She had scarcely eaten, was unkempt, and had refused, after one vain search, ever to come upstairs, even to the dining-room floor, and this though every attention had been bestowed on her. I have noticed a curious thing when she has kittens—that she graduates the size of the mice she brings them, half-stunning the mice first; but even so, the kittens appear terribly afraid of their new plaything, and for some time dare not take part in the game. Is this universally true? Is the taste for mice a cultivated one? The taste for fish must surely be, since cats could never have caught them for themselves; their fondness for shell-fish is especially puzzling, as they are quite unable to get at the meat without aid. Have we here a clear case of inherited instincts?

One more question. Has any one ever attempted to breed a special race of cats, for special characteristics, as has been done with dogs? If not, is it fair to compare the intelligence of one with the other? For centuries dogs have been carefully weeded and tended and trained; with cats, do we not begin afresh with each generation, instead of guarding the race with care and strengthening by selection their good points? Thanking you for the pleasure your animal studies have given me, in common with your many other readers.—I am, Sir, &c.,

ROSA M. BARRETT

June 29, 1895.

A JEALOUS CAT.

SIR,—May I add to your animal stories a striking instance of that spirit of jealousy which insists on all or none? I had a cat which had long been an inmate of the house, and received all the attentions which it is well known old maids lavish on such animals. Finding the mice were more than one cat could attend to, I secured a kitten, and wished to keep the two. My cat was indignant, and in very plain language requested the kitten to go. I endeavoured to make peace, lifted both on to the table, and expostulated with puss. She listened with a sullen expression, and then suddenly gave a claw at the kitten's eye. I scolded and beat her, upon which she left the house and I never saw her again.—I am, Sir, &c.,   DOROTHEA BEALE.

July 27, 1895.

THE CAT THAT UNDERSTOOD.

SIR,—I am induced to send you an account of a remarkable instance of feline sagacity which occurred in my house last week. About a fortnight ago my black Persian cat brought to the house a young sparrow, and taking it to the front door-mat, began stripping it of its feathers. The cook not approving of the litter made by the said feathers, doubled the mat over, and told the cat he must not make such a litter, but strew the feathers on the wrong side of the mat, and not on the top. A fortnight subsequent to this lecture the cat brought in another bird, and, marvellous to say, himself turned the mat (which was a heavy coir mat) over with his claws, and littered the wrong side of it with the feathers, precisely as the cook had told him to do. This is absolutely true. If it had been told me as a story, I should have been very sceptical as to its truth. But I have witnesses by ocular proof as to its being a fact and without exaggeration.—I am, Sir, &c.,

H. D.

August 17, 1895.

A FELINE MOURNER.

SIR,—I read with much interest the stories of animals, especially cats, which appear from time to time in the *Spectator.* May I add one showing that these much-maligned animals have both memory and affection? I had a dear little dog, a Skye-terrier, and some time after he came to my house a wandered cat was added to the establishment. He was very kind to "Bessie," as we called our new inmate, and watched over her with great care, never allowing her to go out by the front door, but pushing her gently in when she attempted it; but they had many a romp together in the back garden. My dog died at the good old age of thirteen, and the cat mourned him like a human being, losing all her liveliness, and moping about the house. About a year after the dog's death I desired the gardener to put turf over his grave, as the house was let, and I feared strangers might dig there. To do this he began to level the earth over the grave, and whenever the cat saw him digging there she got into a most excited state, frisking about in the wildest spirits, evidently expecting that her kind companion was to be restored to her.

Her disappointment, when he never appeared, was trying to witness ; and she has been a " sadder and a wiser " cat ever since, doing her duty faithfully by the mice, but apparently expecting little pleasure in life.—I am, Sir, &c., L. S.

August 17, 1895.

A CAT WITH A FIRE-BRIGADE MEDAL.

SIR,—A lady friend of mine had a very favourite cat, named " Peter." One night she left him in his usual sleeping-place, and went to her own room. Not long after she heard a noise at her door—scratching and other sounds, which she knew must come from the cat—and took no notice of it at first; but as it continued, she opened her door, upon which the cat immediately turned and walked down straight to the kitchen, followed by his mistress, who, to her dismay, saw that the legs of the table were on fire! She started at once to the station of the fire-brigade—not waiting for bonnet or shawl—(about five minutes' walk). The engine came and extinguished the fire, and the fire-brigade presented the cat with a medal, which it wore always hung round its neck. This took place in Brighton. The station of the fire-brigade is in West Hill Road, where this story can be verified. The cause of the fire was traced to the fact of the fire in the grate having been raked out as usual, some of the hot cinders had reached the wood-flooring, and the table was not far off.—I am, Sir, &c.,

ESTHER WELLS.

August 31, 1895.

A BIRD AND CAT CATASTROPHE.

SIR,—Here is the story of a cat and a bird. Two young ladies dwelt together,—one the owner of a canary, which she petted and played with ; the other was the mistress of a beautiful cat, which was nursed and patted and petted also. They were a happy and united family. The owner of the cat went abroad for a time, and pussy grew sad and melancholy, and at last became jealous of the bird, which was daily petted as usual, while she was sadly neglected. Pussy could not, and would not, stand this treatment ; her jealousy grew day by day till at last, in a fit of rage, she made a dash at the little bird and tore him limb from limb. Then seized by remorse she fled, but the owner of the bird was frantic, and she beat the cat and mourned for her bird ; and the owner of the cat when she heard of the catastrophe shed sad tears, not, indeed, because the bird was dead, but because her pussy had been beaten ; and so the peace of that happy family was destroyed for a time. Pussy, overwhelmed with remorse at the crime she had committed, was found the next day curled up and asleep in the little bird's cage. Now, the problem for psychologists required to be solved is, why did that cat go into that cage ?   The only solution that suggests itself to the persons concerned is, that by going there she thought she might regain the favour of the mistress whose happiness she had so ruthlessly destroyed, by taking the place of the bird, and so, perhaps, in due time, be changed into a little petted bird herself.—I am, Sir, &c.,   CATALONIA.

October 19, 1895.

'" BUFF."

Sir,—I have read with interest for many years the dog-stories in the *Spectator*, therefore I will contribute to your pages, with your permission, an instance of sagacity in a large and very handsome Persian cat, which came to my knowledge recently while staying at Bar Harbour, Maine. The maid who fed " Buff," and for whom he seemed to have most affection, was in the habit of putting out the lamps in the parlour, where " Buff" slept on a rug in the corner, after we retired. He is tall enough, when standing on his hind feet, to rattle the knob of the door with his paw,—and this is his usual way of asking to be let in. Just as Jennie was going to bed, she heard this sound, and when she opened the door, he mewed and ran toward the stairs ; she followed him to the parlour, and perceived at once it was to put out the lamps she was called. As soon as she had done this, he laid down content. How much reasoning did this action on the cat's part imply ?—I am, Sir, &c.,

M. S. T.

October 26, 1895.

BIRDS.

ROOKS.

MY TAME ROOK.

Sir,—The eccentric behaviour of the tame ravens described in your last number appears to be characteristic of their tribe. I have for some time had in my possession a tame rook, whose pranks and oddities are a constant source of amusement to me, and not unfrequently of annoyance to others. "Poppy," when quite young, and still hardly able to fly, was found in our garden, which is quite in the town, and surrounded by streets, and a noisy factory. How he got there, we never discovered; but being there, he has never left us. At first he was kept in a large cage; and when I let him out, I held him by a long string attached to his leg. But as he escaped several times, and yet always came back at my call, this constraint was soon abandoned, and perfect liberty allowed him. He never leaves our garden, flies about at will, roosts in the stable, and will come into the house whenever allowed. But so mischievous is he, that he has of late been carefully excluded. He leads the cook a life,—the other day he was found in the act of carrying a hen's egg off the kitchen table. Last summer, while we were all away from home, "Poppy" was sent to some friends about thirty miles off. There he lived in exactly the same style, seeming no whit disturbed by the change of place or people, and at the end of a month was brought back here again.

We have also two cats and a dog, "Scrub," an Airedale terrier, who live in considerable awe of "Poppy," as he frequently attacks them, steals their food, and otherwise maltreats them. None of us would much care to take a bone away from "Scrub," but "Poppy," after slyly pecking his tail to attract his attention, darts at the bone and carries it off in triumph. Apparently for the sake of teasing him, "Poppy" has practised and perfected an imitation of his bark, which is so good that I am often puzzled to know whether it be "Scrub" or "Poppy" who is speaking. Only the other day, the cry of one of the cats called my attention to the fact that "Poppy" was hauling away at his tail, and dragging him step by step down the slope of the lawn. "Poppy will also playfully attack children, pecking their legs, and pulling their dress. In his feeding he is almost om- nivorous. The other day, alas! he forgot himself so far as to burst open the guinea-pigs' cage, and kill and eat one of the little ones. Do rooks usually eat small animals?

As I have never heard before of a tame rook, I thought that perhaps some account of this most interesting bird might interest your readers. I can, however, hardly claim to be his tamer, as from his first appearance he showed himself most friendly and sociable. A week or two ago, I was obliged to clip his wings, but only to prevent him entering the bedrooms and making havoc there.—I am, Sir, &c.,

KATHARINE H. HODGKINSON.

July 12, 1890.

"JACKO."

SIR,—But for a way I have of never doing to-day what I can do to-morrow, you would have received long ago an account of my tame rook, for I have always intended that "Jacko" should, if possible, be honoured with a place in the *Spectator*. But though through my procrastination "Poppy" has forestalled him, possibly you will generously find room for both, especially if I can make it appear that "Jacko" is the more interesting bird of the two. And so, to begin with, did "Poppy" ever build a nest? "Jacko" built a splendid one—in an apple-tree, and in the autumn—two or three years ago ; and for no ostensible purpose, unless he intended to ask the tame jackdaw—a charming little bird that always called itself "John-John"—to share it with. him, and between whom and "Jacko" there was a strong affection. I must have had him quite five years before, much to my astonishment, it occurred to him to build. I was sitting on the lawn one afternoon, and had noticed "Jacko" march past me two or three times, always with a stick in his beak ; so at last I followed him, and found him hard at work trying to

lay the foundations of a nest! He was quite a fortnight over that wonderful nest, though every morning,
directly he was loose (he sleeps in a cage in the
greenhouse), he began to work, and never stopped,
except for his meals, till, quite tired out, he went to
his cage at night. I got quite sorry for him, and
tried to help him sometimes by holding up sticks to
him one at a time, which he took from my hand as
he wanted them. When at last the nest was finished,
he often had his afternoon nap in it. " John-John "
would never look at it.

There is a small rookery here, and " Jacko " this
year, instead of building on his own account, tried to
help the wild rooks, following them about with twigs
in his beak, and keeping with them all day, often
running after them on the lawn with some of his
dinner in his beak, wanting to feed them as he fed
" John-John "; but they snubbed him dreadfully.
One day poor, social " Jacko " must have thought he
had at last found a responsive companion ; for he
had flown into one of the bedrooms, and was found
bowing and cawing to the rook in the looking-glass !
And more than once since then, he has been met
going upstairs with some delicacy in his beak, evidently intended for his shadowy love.

Being interested in " Poppy," I should like to suggest
that there may be danger in his having his wings
clipped. " Jacko's " were at one time, but never since
the day when a neighbour's cat was found in the very
act of carrying him off, and when nothing but poor
" Jacko's " loud protest against the proceeding—which

was heard in the house—saved him. Now he can fly almost as well as any of the wild rooks, and so is safe from any such danger. "Poppy's" mistress writes that they never discovered where he came from, but he would almost certainly come from the nearest rookery. Properly the young rooks do not come to the ground till they can fly well and are quite independent ; it is the poor, forlorn little things that come down too soon that develop into "tame rooks," being altogether dependent upon those who chance to pick them up. I speak from sad experience, for they come down so persistently here, that I sometimes think the old birds —"impatient of the worry of them," as, alas! has been written lately of other parents—bundle them over the edge of the nest. I think them quite clever enough to do this, and also to have discovered that the greenhouse here is a kind of foundling hospital, where their cast-out little ones will be sure of a home. In most rookeries the disposal of the young birds is a very simple affair,—the sportsman is ready with his gun as soon as the young rooks are ready for flight. I was calling one afternoon on a friend, when a lady I did not know came in, and as she also had a rookery, my friend told her of mine, and said how fond I was of the rooks. "Ah!" said the lady, "so am I ; I often say that through the season we almost live on rook-pie." And when I suggested that I should not like to see my rooks in a pie, her really delightful answer was : "No ; some people prefer them stewed."

I am writing this letter on the lawn, and "Jacko," after having walked up and down it with me for some time, is now perched on the garden bench near me, and pretending to be asleep; but in reality he is wanting to get possession of my letter, and if I were to turn away for a moment, off he would fly with it, for, like " Poppy," " Jacko " is a terrible thief.   I wish I could tell him the contents of it, and get him to add a postscript.—I am, Sir, &c.,   S. W.

July 19, 1890.

THE ROOK.

SIR,—Your lady-correspondent from Trinity Vicarage, Gainsborough, asks if any instance can be given similar to that of her tamed rook. I can give one such, which I had on the 3rd of last month from Mrs. Cole, of Condover Hall, near Shrewsbury, as follows :—

" I have an old rook which I found on the road-side three years ago, with a gunshot wound in his side and one wing quite blown off. He seemed very old and wild, but I brought him home, and though left completely at liberty in a tree in the garden, he has never failed to eat out of my hand, then, at once, and ever since, and shows the most extraordinary devotion and great intelligence."

In the same letter, she also sent two other accounts of a kestrel hawk and a rat, which I have had copied to add to that of the rook, in case you may be able to find room for them, as I think they may be as interesting to some of your readers as they were to me. They show what may be done with animals and birds by kindness, and are much to the credit of the writer of the letter. I must add that I asked her for leave to make use of them as I might have opportunity, and had her ready assent to my doing so. She wrote :—

"I see in your book on 'British Birds,' you state that the kestrel is easily tamed. Our bird was taken from a nest last year, and put into a cage out of doors, for a few days only, until fledged. He was then turned out, and flew across the park into the woods, and was seen no more for some days, when he returned, found his way into the house, and has never voluntarily left it since. We often turn him out, and see him a mile or more from the house, but soon after find him searching for an open window by which he may reach the dining-room, where he lives by preference, perching on a picture-frame, but always coming on to my husband's arm when called, even though with thirty people at dinner, and through the glare of lamps and candles. He invariably twitters a sort of soft song when we speak to him. He is a grand bird, in perfect plumage." . . . "I have a white rat, who lives, as all our pets do, entirely loose in the house or garden, perfectly free to leave us if they choose. The rat was given to me as old and worthless two years ago, then quite wild. He gradually became extremely tame, and during a severe illness I had last year, he took it into his head to sit on my pillow to guard me. Ever since then, he has continued to sleep there ; he runs upstairs with me, and follows me to bed, sleeping always on the bolster or pillow by my head. He is very plucky, and defended himself during one whole night when he was shut up accidentally in the same room with a large and savage cat. He was found sitting up, with teeth and claws ready, and was perfectly overjoyed when his human friends took him up. Though six months have elapsed, nothing will induce him to enter that room again. Our dogs are perfect friends with him. He uses his left paw always when drinking, 'ladling' the water up to his mouth, even from the bottom of a tumbler, and is quite 'left-handed.'"

I may perhaps add the following account of a rook, or rather of two rooks, which I sent to *Land and Water* some years back :—

" I read with much interest in your last issue, in Mr. Reid's communication, the following passage :— 'I observed a curious thing one day lately. Some food by some good Christian had been thrown out to the starving birds, when a rook came down and flew back to where he had left another rook sitting in a very weak-looking condition, and fed her with what he had picked up. This he did twice in my sight before taking anything to himself. It was a very interesting sight, and I was very much pleased with it.' "

I was particularly struck with this because I had some time previously received from a correspondent in Wales, a stranger to me, a precisely similar account of another of these birds :—

" What I wanted to mention was this. One day, in the bitterest of the weather, when I am sure our friend the rook I have spoken of was indeed reduced to great extremities, the bird nevertheless performed the following good deed. It picked up a bit of bread, carried it to another rook, which sat on the terrace wall, too shy to come nearer, and fed it there. Nor was this after having satisfied its own hunger, for it had only just alighted."

When I put this little story down, I had a misgiving that any one who might read it would scarcely be disposed to believe it, as beyond credibility. I was therefore much gratified at having so soon afterwards seen such an exactly similar fact recorded in corroboration of it, as above. It was indeed, I think, a very touching incident, and one to make every one, I should hope, who reads it, have much good feeling for all God's creatures.—I am, Sir, &c.,

F. O. MORRIS.

August 2, 1890.

A COLONY OF ROOKS.

SIR,—Last year you were good enough to publish some letters of mine on the above subject, which, judging from the number of questions I received from many, seem to have proved interesting. May I say, in continuation of the subject, that the rooks have appeared in the same place this year ; but, whereas last year they came with great din and proclamation and quarrelling as then described, this year they literally sneaked in by degrees, and commenced to build quietly without the slightest noise ? Can it be that the hardships of the winter and the present cold have been too much for them, and have effectually cooled down their natural demonstrativeness ?—I am, Sir, &c.,   W. H. W. H.

March 21, 1891.

ROOKS IN THE CORN.

SIR,—In the *Spectator* of May 6th, your correspondent, "A Member of the Society for the Protection of Birds," mentions the usefulness of rooks in a cornfield. An old farmer near us is a great friend to the rooks and never allows them to be destroyed, since a day "years ago," when he shot a bird busy among his fresh-sown fields, and, on opening it, found its crop to be full of wireworms. For some time after this incident, "the boys" continued to bring home dead rooks as the spoil of their guns; but the old man insisted on each being opened, and on every occasion the birds were found to have fed solely on grubs.

We have a large rookery, and, needless to say, never allow them to be disturbed, much to the indignation of a young neighbouring farmer, who declared we should ruin him by our ill-timed humanity. Two years ago, he sowed a large field with wheat, and the operation was no sooner completed than the acreage was black with our rooks. The wrathful owner was in despair, and was advised to plant some other crop on the land, which must of necessity be quite barren of seed ; but, to punish us for our folly, he determined to " let the land alone till autumn." He did so, and never reaped a richer harvest. Since then he has " taken note " of the ways of rooks, and believes, with us, that they do more good than harm. Our birds build close to our kitchen-garden, and are regularly fed on the lawn, like fowls, all winter ; and we never even miss a potato. It is said that rooks will follow their friends. This spring we temporarily removed to a house a mile beyond our own property, and three couples of our rooks have taken up their abode in the elm-trees close to our new quarters, and are busy rearing families, and constantly coming to the windows to be fed, as this extremely dry season pro-bably sends the worms and grubs below the sub-soil, and out of reach of their beaks.—I am, Sir, &c.,

ANOTHER MEMBER OF THE SOCIETY FOR
THE PROTECTION OF BIRDS.
(New Forest Branch.)

May 20, 1893.

THE HABITS OF ROOKS.

SIR,—Can any of your numerous readers who are lovers of natural history throw light upon the laws and government of that curious commonwealth, a large rookery? Have the rooks leaders who head their columns when they sally forth at dawn, north, south, east, and west, in so orderly and purposeful a manner, and who marshal the returning hosts in the evening?

I have had the opportunity of observing the ways of the inhabitants of one of the largest rookeries in the West-country, and their systematic and unvarying daily routine. In the grey dawn the rooks may be heard holding vociferous council together before starting for their various feeding-grounds, some of which, I am told, are distant more than twenty miles. During the day and until sunset not a single bird is to be seen near home (except in bad weather), so complete is the exodus. The rookery is situated in a belt of lofty beeches and other trees which shelter the beautiful garden in front of a large country house; the corresponding trees on the east and opposite side also receive a proportion of the birds, but only those,

I have noticed, which are crowded out of the more favoured quarters. Every evening when the sun has sunk below the horizon, and the trunks of the beeches stand out black against the orange afterglow, the rooks begin to come home ; first in small companies, when a solitary bird sometimes turns back as if to reconnoitre, but presently in a mighty rush which fills the air with a sound as of waves breaking on shingle, heightened by confused cawings and the sharper note of the numberless jackdaws who live in company with the rooks. The choosing of roosting-places is a long and exciting operation, and many times the whole vast multitude rise again and again in a cloud into the air and swirl round and round the house, literally darkening the sky and filling the air far and near as with a great black snow-storm. It is an extraordinary and most interesting sight, and the dusk has deepened into darkness before the countless myriads have settled down to their liking. In summer, detachments of the rooks, with the young birds, leave the parent-rookery (like swarms of bees) and go into summer quarters elsewhere, all returning home for the winter and spring.—I am, Sir, &c.,

CORNWALL.

October 5, 1895.

THE HABITS OF ROOKS.

SIR,—That these birds are weatherwise I am firmly convinced, and I think, after continual observation of their habits, that they do elect a leader, or leaders, to head their foraging flocks, at any rate ; also, that they have one or more sentinels stationed at various points when they are feeding, who give an alarm when a foe approaches. I was staying some years ago at a seaside place in North Wales, called Beaumaris, where there was a fine old rookery within a short distance of the town, situated near Sir Richard Bulkeley's residence, Baron Hill, and I, being a very early riser, used to watch the rooks of a morning from my bedroom window. They were wont to assemble at daybreak on the shore, and after a brief consultation, one, or sometimes two grave-looking birds, would rise on the wing and mount carefully into the air ; remain there, as if stationary, for a moment, and then fly seaward followed by the whole company. I noticed them cross the Straits in this fashion several times, and was informed by my landlady that they went over the water to some famous sands on the Carnarvonshire side, where cockles and other, to use her expression, "shore refuge," abounded. They returned at night about sunset. After a time I observed that on some fine mornings the leaders, instead of going off towards the Straits, wheeled round, and followed by their suite, flew off to Baron Hill Woods. This puzzled me, until I noticed that, however fine the early part of the day had been, the evening always proved stormy or wet, so I came to the conclusion that rooks were good weather-prophets, foresaw a change of wind, and knew how unwise it would be to go over the water on that day.

I often afterwards had an opportunity of observing the habits of the Anglesea rooks during my stay ; for I took a house on the island, still close to the shore, but some distance from the town, nearer Penmon, and there I have more than once observed rooks feeding amongst the seaweeds left by the receding tide, rise with a shell-fish in their beak to a considerable height, then drop it on the rocks, and descend to pick the fish out of the shell they had so cleverly broken. Mussels seemed to be their particular vanity, but these seaside rooks would eat all kinds of small mollusca. Rooks inland are also slightly carnivorous. I have seen them in severe winters pick bones like magpies, which I have thrown out to them—some of the " Selborne rooks," as I call them ; for we have not a rookery very near Liss—came here to be fed. I really flattered myself that I had won the confidence of three of them ; for they came regularly every day quite close to the windows, to look for bones and pieces of bread, and without their usual guard, too.

When they come in a flock, to look for wireworms amongst the young corn in an adjoining field, I always see a black gentleman or two on some tall oak-trees in the field close to this house, waiting to give the danger signal if a man armed appears. I do believe that they must know the gun is an engine of destruction. I could relate more about rooks and jackdaws, but fear this letter is already too long to be received with favour.—I am, Sir, &c.,

HELEN E. WATNEY.

October 19, 1895.

THE HABITS OF ROOKS.

SIR,—Your correspondent's letter, in the *Spectator* of October 5th, about rooks leads me to tell you an incident which always seems to me one of the strangest of the many stories of the sagacity of rooks. We were living some years ago in the suburbs of London, and had a garden in which were a good many fine old elms. They grew in an irregular line down the length of the lawn, and were continued beyond the boundary hedge half-way across the field beyond. The trees in the field were full of rooks' nests, and were a perpetual interest and amusement to watch—but never a nest was built in the trees on our side the hedge till we had been for some years in the house. Then one day we found the rooks had begun a nest in one of our trees, a fine old elm under which we constantly sat and a favourite spot for after-noon tea. This we found was too inconvenient to be borne, as we could no longer sit there, and much as we loved our neighbours, the rooks, we felt they must have notice to quit; so, before the nest was finished, I took my husband's revolver and fired through the empty nest. The effect was immense. The whole colony gathered and flew round and round the tree, making a great noise for a long time, and within a few hours they removed every twig of the nearly completed nest and rebuilt it, this time in the next tree, which was only a few yards distant, but grew on the other side of the hedge. They never trespassed again. After some years we left the house, and the move took place just at the time the rooks were beginning to build. About ten days after we left, I returned to the old house for a few hours, and found to my astonishment that the rooks were in full possession of our garden, and had already made five or six nests in the trees on our lawn, some of them close to the house. The gardener was still at work, and a caretaker with children in the house, so that it was not the greater quiet that tempted them.—I am, Sir, &c.,   A. E. THOMPSON.

October 19, 1895.

THE HABITS OF ROOKS.

SIR,—The rookery here is of considerable antiquity, although at first sight it is not easy to see what has so endeared it to the birds. The grove wherein they build is reputed to have been planted shortly after the Restoration. The trees are placed on a steep hillside facing Dartmoor, and having run up very high, their frail, mastlike stems sway in heavy storms with exciting oscillations. Dartmoor and its outskirts is a treeless region, and probably many years after my ancestress had put in her young trees, the great rarity of shelter elsewhere fixed the affection of the first builders. Subsequently, and all through this century, the inland combes and hillsides have grown more wooded, yet no thought of less storm-tossed homes seems to tempt our friends of many generations to leave us. One notable trait is their eminent preference for the beech-tree. The lime and other native trees they tolerate. But new-fangled firs and such-like they will not abide, although they are very ready to use the towering top of a silver-fir as a spying-post for their sentinels. And how wise their instinct was has been abundantly made clear to us, for in the great blizzard some years ago, while the aged beeches bent like whips and lived, the heavily clad firs toppled and perished.

Every one has heard that rooks hate being crowded, and so we have found out. A good many years back, my father, having rather neglected their feelings, and kept back his ukase for the triennial massacre of the youngsters, a great deal of bad blood arose. There was much discussion and some conflict ; the upshot of which was that a certain number (presumably young birds) were ostracised. These outcasts took up their abode in a humbler beech-grove, within a gunshot of the house ; and there until quite lately a few nests have steadily been built. But the movement was never very successful; and now that the home-rookery has been depleted by the recent stormy winters, and by a somewhat severe slaughter, it is evident that the exiles will be received back. In the year, however, subsequent to the first expulsion, stronger measures seemed required by the rulers of the rooks, and an unheard-of thing, a colony, was despatched to the churchyard avenue of limes, a mile away. The undertaking was bold and statesmanlike; but in a few years it ceased to be. No self-respecting rook could bear the meanness and stress of village life, after having tasted the solemn solitude of its native grove, or build in limes when beeches were to be had. So the churchyard knows them no more.

The movements of our Queen from Windsor to Osborne, and Osborne to Balmoral, are not more regular than those of the rooks. Once the breeding-time is well over, and the young fledglings capable of something more than flapping round from bough to bough, comes a season of happy excursions. Then presently the swaying trees are free day and night of the busy chatter and solemn cawings they have been alive with for previous weeks. All the summer days, out in the heart of the solitary moors, guarded for the most part by some reverend elder perched on any handy granite boulder, the gregarious tribe pursues its pleasures and its food—unless tempted inland by the riches of the cultivated fields. All the summer evenings in ordered array they fly down from the Tors, straight across the leafy canopy of their beloved grove, nor stay their pinions until they come to their summer bed-chambers in a richly wooded valley some six miles westward. Now, when autumn is well advanced, they are returning to their rookery. Every evening, of late, I have seen their sentinel perched on the topmost bough of a silver-fir. With true military instinct the vedette is usually posted on a lofty tree which has begun to die downward. So the sentinel sees and is seen with greater freedom, and there is no doubt as to his office.

Such have been the habits of the birds so long as I can recall, and such, I doubt not, they will remain until some fierce winter gale uproots their habitation. In the meantime the owner of their grove is anxiously contriving a fresh beechen home for his sable neighbours. But it does not at all follow that the rooks will consent to approve his efforts.—I am, Sir, &c.,

V. W. CALMADY HAMLYN.

November 9, 1895.

THE HABITS OF ROOKS.

SIR,—Rooks must either have very keen sight or
very keen scent. I have frequently passed near a
flight of rooks settled on a field, with a stick in my
hand ; but I could never get near them with a gun
in my hand. To test the matter, I have aimed at
them with the stick, but they remained perfectly
unconcerned. Can it be that they smell the powder ?
I am inclined to think it was sight after all, for I do
not remember that I approached them any more
easily from the leeward.—I am, Sir, &c.,

W. F. HERBERT.

November 9, 1895.

THE HABITS OF ROOKS.

SIR,—For nine years I lived under the shadow of a rookery, and took notes of proceedings there. It was not a very old one, but a recent offshoot (I was told) from the ancient one of Hankshead Hall at the foot of the hill, where part of the buildings, granary and mill, erected by the monks of Furness, stand to this day. There the rooks' trees were compact, flat-topped oaks, while with us they were mostly beech-trees; and I had the idea (mistaken, perhaps) that the birds only took to the beeches, planted about the avenue to a house nearly five hundred feet above the sea-level, because no other large trees were to be had in the neighbourhood. For it was noticeable that while the beech-grove was itself larger, they used every other odd kind of tree that happened to be against it. On the north side of the house the farm-buildings were shut out by a compact clump of mixed trees—wych-elms, horse-chestnuts, sycamore, spruce, and larch. Every one of these trees was used by the rooks, the two spruces and the sycamore particularly, containing a great many nests each. On the avenue, or south side, where the beeches were, they tried at different times to nest in a Spanish chestnut, a lime, and a hornbeam, all of them tall, spindly specimens, pressed in by the beeches. These attempts, however, were not repeated ; and the increase of nests in the beeches was gradual but firm, with the increase of the colony. A computation gave the total number of nests as (at least) sixteen in 1887 ; and were by 1894 as many (at least) as fifty. The difficulty in counting lay in the (apparently) double nests, which often in the spruce-fir and the beech were backed up against each other. Indeed, I came to the conclusion that the rooks loved a semi-detached residence ; while the establishment of a nest on an out-standing tree—as in a fine, lonely sycamore by the back gate—was always resisted by the colony.

Often in spring gales there were calamities in the rookery. The one of April 28, 1892, coming so late, when eggs were laid and hard set—and even chipped —was peculiarly disastrous. I remember picking up and turning over the fallen nests in the shrubbery, with their contents shattered, hard by (some of them were weighty with old linings that had attained a peat-like consistency). And all I could find were blown from beech-trees, none were on the north side, though, of course, some may have been wrecked that did not fall. When the storm had subsided and the happier rooks were at ease again, and not clinging, distraught, to the wind-tossed boughs of the more sheltered trees, it was a curious and pitiful sight to see some rooks (to the number of about double the wretched nests) withdrawn from the noisy nursery to a lonely fell-side ash, where they perched in solemn stillness. Whatever the worth of the beech-tree as a nest-site for the rooks, it is certain that the beechen-bough is in great favour with them as nest-material. For the builders continually break the tender, pliant, sometimes forked, twig-ends and carry them off to lay and twine into that basket form that only the sap-filled twig will take.—I am, Sir, &c,

MARY L. ARMITT.

November 30, 1895.

ROOKS.

SIR,—The following account of some manœuvres or an army of rooks in Normandy may be of interest to some of your readers. Early in this month I was passing along the valley of the river Eure, in Normandy, when I stopped to watch the proceedings of these rooks, which were assembling in large quantities on the low hills on the left side of the little river-valley. As the rooks flew in from all sides to this rendezvous, they settled down on the hill-side in six separate bodies or regiments, each regiment being separated from those on either side of it by a distance of some fifty to a hundred yards. In this position they remained, till apparently all the rooks had arrived. When the last late-comers had settled down, however, a band of ten or twelve flew up from the first regiment—that is to say, the one which had taken up its position nearest the spot where I was standing, and which was on the extreme right of the line. This body then flew away in the direction away from the river—presumably to search the country for other stragglers, for in a few minutes they returned, their number increased to seventeen or so. No sooner had these last settled down, than a single rook got up from the first regiment, and started to fly down the line, causing an immense clamour of cawing as he went ; having reached the farther end, the sixth regiment—as I must call it, for want of a better term —the sixth regiment rose into the air as one rook, and flew down into the valley, to settle in the trees forming an avenue on each side of the river. The aide-de-camp rook then commenced his flight back along the line, and as he repassed, each of the remaining regiments, one after another, rose separately into the air, and flew down to the trees by the river, where they all settled down for the night.—I am, Sir, &c.,

G. P. D.

November 30, 1895.

CUCKOOS.

THE CUCKOO AND ITS FOSTER-MOTHER.

SIR,—Seeing that natural history finds a place in the *Spectator*, I venture to send you the following incident in bird-life, a common occurrence of course, but perhaps not often witnessed. I am occupying a house in the valley of the Itchen, and looking out the other morning from my bedroom window, I observed a large bird squatting listlessly on the gravel-walk below. I wondered what it could be; it was neither blackbird, thrush, nor turtle-dove, which latter, at first sight, it resembled. Presently my difficulty was solved; another bird appeared on the scene; the first was a young, fully fledged cuckoo, the other, a water-wagtail, his foster-mother; and never was offspring more tenderly nurtured. Throughout the day the cuckoo might constantly be seen, either on the ground, tree, or fence near by, the stolid recipient of every insect the little bird, running, flying, and fluttering hither and thither, could catch and carry to the insatiable maw of her changeling. When the cuckoo was on the ground, she ran up to him, and, standing on tip-toe, placed the food in his mouth ; when seated on the fence, she perched on his back, and the cuckoo, turning his head, received the dainty morsel. At first he remained for a quarter of an hour or so in the same place and position, then he and his foster-mother would fly off together ; he to light on tree or fence, and she to minister to his wants as before ; later he became more lively, and hopped about after the running water-wagtail ; then he withdrew himself from public gaze, among the trees and shrubs, the wagtail still continuing to feed' him.. The pair were first observed on the 4th inst., but since the 21st we think that he is gone, for we imagine we can identify the foster-mother from that date, seeking her own living, trotting about the lawn with nothing to distract her, but whether in sadness at the loss, or joy at being relieved from the care of her exacting child, who can say ? *We* congratulate the wee thing on her emancipation.—I am, Sir, &c.,

ALFRED BONHAM-CARTER.

August 29, 1891.

THE CUCKOO.

SIR, — May I supplement your correspondent's account of the cuckoo by our own experience this summer ? A wagtail built in the ivy on our school chapel, and laid, as we supposed, six eggs. Much as I wished for one for our collection, I felt that the nest was too much " in sanctuary," and left them alone ; and one Sunday all but one were hatched. This last came out on Monday evening, and on Tuesday morning I visited the nest ; and behold! all but one of the young ones were dead—some on the ground, and some in the nest. I called for my brother, and he and the gardener came up and took the survivor, which was quite a different colour, and much bigger than the corpses, out of the nest, and my brother at once said it must be a cuckoo. So it proved to be, and was for three weeks a great source of interest and amusement to us all, especially as it grew and fledged ; and the boys were taken to see it most days in detachments. The poor little wagtails had a hard time of it, as it had an enormous appetite. I tried to help them by feeding it twice a day with chopped-up egg, which the little monster swallowed voraciously down its huge and bright-orange throat. It grew to about the size of a pigeon, and one evening, on being a little teased, it suddenly flew away, and was only seen once again on the railing, with the patient wag-tails still supplying it with food.—I am, Sir, &c.,

E. E. B

September 12, 1891.

AN HONEST CUCKOO.

SIR,—The following instance of unusual conduct on
the part of this bird may, I think, interest your
readers. I copy it from the *Bristol Times and Mirror*
of yesterday :—

  "Westerman's *Moaats Hefte* contains an account
by Professor Adolf Müller of a cuckoo who, abandon-
ing the dishonest practice of her species, hatched and
reared her young. On May 16, 1888, Herr Müller
was crossing a wood, when a cuckoo started almost
from under his feet. He examined the ground carefully, and discovered beneath a tussock of grass, in a
little hollow, three eggs. The first was light-yellow
with brown spots ; the second, orange with greenish
lines ; the third, smaller than the others, was of a
greenish-gray with minute red spots and blotches of
reddish-brown. The Professor, with true German
patience, came every day, and, by the aid of an opera-
glass, observed, without disturbing her, the habits of
the extraordinary bird which chance had revealed to
him. She proceeded to sit with irreproachable regularity. In ten days a young one was hatched. The
mother abandoned the two sterile eggs, and devoted

herself to the little cuckoo, whom she sheltered under her wings in the keen morning air, and supplied with caterpillars from a neighbouring oak-copse. In three weeks it could fly, whereas under the care of foster-parents young cuckoos do not master that accomplishment until after the lapse of six or seven weeks. A noteworthy fact in the discovery is that the cuckoo can lay eggs of different sizes and colours."

This is certainly a very unusual occurrence, and one which it would be interesting to have verified. Perhaps some of your readers may have heard of it before, or you, Sir, may know of the paper *Moaats Hefte*, and whether the account is likely to be worthy of credence?—I am, Sir, &c., R. L. BOWLEY

August 13, 1892.

THE CUCKOO.

SIR,—Your correspondent, Mr. Bowley, after quoting the case of a cuckoo which hatched and reared its own young, asks if " any of your readers have heard of this case before." I, for one, am familiar with it, but unfortunately my ornithological books are all in Edinburgh, and I cannot refer to the case; but I think it is given in the last edition of Garrell, which shows that the author believed Herr Müller to be a trustworthy authority. I confess, however, I do not remember the statement that this particular young cuckoo was able to fly in less than half the usual time. It is singular that all the American cuckoos hatch and rear their own eggs, whilst the myriads of American starlings (a closely allied bird) are all parasitical.

I would not, however, have ventured to trouble you as to the cuckoo were it not that its name suggests to me the most obscure of all questions of bird-life, that of migration. I think I have read nearly all that English ornithologists have said on the subject, and in my humble opinion not one of them have fairly grappled with this most mysterious circumstance in the life of birds. One writer after another, with almost cuckoo similarity of voice, tells us that summer migrants leave us when their special food becomes scarce, and when cold reminds them of bright winter homes. They tell us—and in this case truly—that when they cross seas they follow lines of flight that their ancestors pursued thousands of years ago, when there was no sea there to cross, and before man was introduced into the world. Thus there are well-known lines of flight across the Mediterranean which the same species of birds have followed for unknown ages. No doubt the design of Providence was to preserve species by causing them to seek warmth and food when the places of their nativity grew cold and fruit-less. But for all that, birds leave us in autumn at certain seasons quite irrespective of cold or want of food, just as bees frequently seek their hibernaculum while the weather is still mild, and emerge from them in spring, though the weather may be colder than when they went to hibernate.

But the question I wish to ask naturalists regards the migration of the *young* cuckoo. It sees the light, let us say, in this remote island (and they are very numerous here). It never saw its parents. These leave us in August, but their unseen offspring remain till September, and even till October. What guides them along the very lines their parents took a month before? What do they know of the lines of flight pursued over dry land ages ago? Is it some hereditary influence (of which the bird is as ignorant as we are), which burns in its brain, and sends it forth in darkness and without a guide or compass to follow the old but to it unknown flight from Northern Europe to join its kindred in distant Africa?

Perhaps science is utterly baffled, and cannot improve upon Addison, who said: "Migration is a direct impulse from the Almighty."—I am, Sir, &c.,

R. SCOT SKIRVING.

August 27, 1892.

THE HONEST CUCKOO.

SIR,—I turned with as great expectation to the letter from Mr. Scot Skirving about the cuckoo in your last issue as I did to that published in the *Spectator* of August 13th, headed " An Honest Cuckoo." But I was destined to quite as much disappointment. The causes of my disappointment were these :—

1. The matter referred to by your correspondent, Mr. Bowley, of August 13th, was not new to me by any means. The first note of the observations of Herr Adolf Müller was not given in " Westermann's Monatshefte " (not " Moaatshefte "), but in the *Gartenlaube ;* and from the *Gartenlaube* an admirable free translation was made some time ago in the *Ibis*—an English repository of facts in ornithology—by a most competent ornithologist. The more recent German note gave rise to paragraphs in London papers, the *Echo* amongst others, from which the *Bristol Times and Mirror* no doubt copied ; and seeing you have so often had to make claims against provincial papers for getting the credit of your own paragraphs, you will, no doubt, be pleased to do this justice to the *Echo*, whose egg has, cuckoo-like, been dropped into the nest of the Bristol paper.

2. I expected some further light from the letter in your last issue which I did not get, and light for which I am eager, and would most heartily welcome.

The notion that the cuckoo sometimes hatches its own eggs is old.   Dr. Erasmus Darwin expressed his belief, based on observation, that this was so ; and he supported his position by quoting a letter from the Rev. Mr. Wilmot, of Morley, near Derby, describing an instance of a cuckoo hatching its own eggs (it could hardly be said to nest, for it simply laid them in a depression among some coal-slack).   This was in 1792.   The cuckoo was first observed by one of Mr. Wilmot's labourers, and was afterwards watched by Mr. Wilmot himself ; and many of his friends came to see the curiosity, among others a Mr. and Mrs. Holyoake.   Mr. Blackwall, the distinguished ornithologist, critically dealt with this case in the *Zoological Journal* for 1829, and came to the conclusion that all were misled, and mistook a night-jar for a cuckoo, which implies more ignorance than can well be believed on the part of a rustic, a country clergyman, and a country gentleman and lady ; since the bristly quills or undeveloped feathers that hang from the upper part of the mouth of the night-jar over the lower are such a striking distinguishing feature, especially when the birds are seen sitting.   Mr. Blackwall's reasons are not wholly convincing—at all events to me.   Since then there have now and again been notes made by observers to the same effect.   The gentleman who writes under the name of " Cannock Brand," in his article on the " Cuckoo " in *Longman's*

Magazine, June, 1891, spoke of one or two instances known to him ; and an Essex naturalist known to me declares an experience of the same kind. It is evident that the cuckoo at one time—though a remote time—nested and brooded its own young, and there is surely no impossibility in reversions to original habit in rare circumstances here, as is found to be. the case in many other instances.

One of the great arguments against the cuckoo brooding is its peculiarity of formation, the stomach lying beneath the sternum ; but—not to speak of the night-jar, which so far shares the peculiarity, and yet hatches its eggs and broods its young—there are the two common North American cuckoos which are so formed, and yet brood their young, one species doing it under a most extraordinary form of communism. "Cannock Brand" gives a case of finding on Wimbledon Common a cuckoo that had laid an egg, or eggs, on the ground, and he came to the conclusion—from what I think was a too narrow basis of facts—that the cuckoo eats its own eggs : a thing which Yarrell (latest edition) will give no countenance to, saying that the notion arises simply from the cuckoo carrying its eggs in its mouth to deposit them in other birds' nests.

Some very noted ornithologists have been inclined to scout the idea of the young cuckoo turning out the true progeny of the foster parents. Within the past few years this has been most carefully observed, and reported with the most exact details, by competent ornithologists—the one the well-known bird painter,

Mrs. Blackburn, and the other the equally well-known Northern ornithologist, Mr. J. Hancock. This proves that, even with experts, it is not safe to dogmatise too much on any point connected with such a vagrant as the cuckoo.

But, the truth is, though I am but an amateur, I am an earnest inquirer on this matter, and would be glad of any further information that can be procured about the cuckoo and its exceptional habits.—I am, Sir, &c.,   ALEXANDER H. JAPP.

September 17, 1892.

AN HONEST CUCKOO.

SIR,—In the *Spectator* of August 13th a correspondent drew your attention to an account, given in "Westermann's Monatshefte," by Professor Adolf Müller, of "an honest cuckoo," who hatched and reared her young. It may interest some of your readers to know that Professor Müller reported a similar case in a most interesting article on the cuckoo's egg, published in 1873 in the *Gartenlaube* (No. 25, p. 407); the main difference being that in this case Professor Müller was not an eye-witness, but relies on the authority of Herr Kiessel, of St. Johann on the Saar, an equally well-known bird-lover.

According to this account, it is proved conclusively by Kiessel and three other eye-witnesses, that towards the end of May, 1868, a cuckoo reared her young in a wood near St. Johann. The bird was discovered by the woodmen sitting on two eggs which lay simply on the ground amid the heath, without any traces of a nest. Kiessel himself observed the bird regularly, and saw that both the eggs were hatched, and the little birds reared with perfect tenderness and care.

These facts, as Müller points out, emphasise the

kinship which exists between our cuckoo and its American cousins, the black-billed or red-eyed cuckoo, and the yellow-billed or rain cuckoo. The latter has, I believe, been seen in England also.—I am, Sir, &c.,

J. B. S. BARRATT.

October 29, 1892.

THE CUCKOO.

SIR,—In your article in the *Spectator* of May 13th
on "Cuckoos and Nightingales," you say that the
popular feeling in England in favour of the cuckoo
is "certainly of recent growth." Is this so certain as
you seem to think it? The earliest reference that I
know to the cuckoo seems to me to express exactly
the common feeling of to-day :—

> " ἦμος κόκκυξ κοκκύζει δρυὸς ἐν πετάλασι
> τὸ πρῶτον, τέρπει δε βροτοὺς ἐπ' ἀπείρονα γαῖαν,"

says Hesiod, who, in "The Works and Days," certainly represents the ordinary feelings of the early
Greek peasant. Moreover, a reference to such well-
known books as Johnson's Dictionary and Masson's
"Three Centuries of English Poetry" will show that
the same feeling prevailed in the days of great
Elizabeth :—

> "The merry cuckoo, messenger of spring,
>   His trumpet shrill hath twice already sounded,"

says Spenser.

" Hark how the jolly cuckoos sing, ·
Cuckoo to welcome in the spring,"

says Lyly, of " Euphues " fame.

" And we hear birds aye tune this merry lay,
Cuckoo, jug-jug, pee-we, to-witta-woo,"

says Thomas Nash.

Have you not allowed your feelings of reprobation of the moral character of the cuckoo to interfere with your judgment as to his pleasant note?—I am, Sir, &c.,   E. F.

May 20, 1893.

STORKS.

SELF-SACRIFICE OF A FEMALE STORK.

SIR,—The animal world abounds in examples of parental affection ; still, the following incident, which I take from a German paper, may interest both your scientific and lay readers. At Neuendorf, in the Teltow district (Prussia), the lightning struck the gable-end of a barn, where a pair of storks had built their nest for years. The flames soon caught the nest, in which the helpless brood was piteously screaming. The mother-stork now protectingly spread out her wings over the young ones, with whom she was burnt alive, although she might have saved herself easily enough by flight. After a short time the male stork returned, and flew for hours in despair round the desolate home.—I am, Sir, &c.,

EIN THIERFREUND.

July 5, 1890.

A STORK'S SELF-SACRIFICE.

SIR,—Your correspondent, "Ein Thierfreund," has given a touching instance of parental affection in his letter on "The Self-Sacrifice of a Female Stork." It is not without parallel. I take the following from Appendix D of Mr. Mark Twain's "Tramp Abroad," which I am sure would interest both your scientific and lay readers :—

" In the daybeforeyesterdayshortlyaftereleveno'clock Night, the inthistownstandingTavern called ' The Waggoner ' was downburnt. When the fire to the onthedownburninghouseresting Stork's Nest reached, flew the parent Storks away. But when the bytheragingfiresurrounded Nest itself caught Fire, straightway plunged the quickreturning MotherStork into the Flames and died, her Wings over her young ones outspread."

This was from a Mannheim journal—I am, Sir, &c.

H. O. D.

July 12, 1890.

A STORK MONOPOLIST.

SIR,—The following incident, illustrating the reasoning faculty in the stork, took place in my Swedish home. It may possibly interest your readers.

In Skane, in the southern part of Sweden, a pair of storks lived for many years on the roof of my father's parsonage. One spring, a pair of young storks appeared in the place, who, after surveying the old nest—probably their parental home—set about building their habitation on the opposite side of the roof. When it was finished and the eggs had been laid, the old female stork returned, took a look at the new-comers, but allowed them to remain in their home in peace. Her attention was soon occupied by a number of young suitors, who zealously wooed her, though she rejected all their offers. Some days later this Penelope among birds was rewarded by the arrival of her old mate. But then came an end to the truce with the young birds. That very evening, the old stork, followed by his female companion, flew to the nest of the new-comers. By violent blows of their beaks they first put the young male stork to flight, and then began to attack the sitting hen. Patiently she suffered all ill-usage and remained upon her eggs. The assailants then altered their tactics. One continued to attack the young mother-bird, while the other, watching till in her struggles to evade the blows an egg became uncovered, instantly pushed it out of the nest. Thus, one by one, the four precious eggs were remorselessly sacrificed. When all the eggs had been destroyed, the young female stork, after standing for some time in the courtyard, looking up to her ruined home as if in despair, sadly flew away. There was never any sign of that pair of storks on our roof again. The old ones had attained their end—henceforth they were the only storks in that part of the country, and were left in sole possession of its food supply. To the inhabitants of our parsonage, whose sympathies for the old storks were thus rudely shaken, it seemed a just retribution that, though the birds had some eggs that summer, none were hatched, and thus the old storks had to return alone to their Southern quarters that winter—a solitary pair !—I am, Sir, &c.,

ANNA GLASELL-ANDERSON.

February 4, 1893.

PARROTS AND CANARIES.

BIRDS AND PICTURES.

SIR,—After reading your correspondent's interest-. ing letter in the *Spectator* of April 20th, about a dog taking notice of a picture, I venture to relate a similar instance. I have a most intelligent tame canary which has the habit of looking at his reflection in a mirror, sometimes singing and dressing his feathers before it. Recently I showed him several coloured pictures of birds ; he immediately came on my finger, sang, pecked at them, and appeared greatly excited. I have frequently tried the same experiment since, and have always succeeded in rousing my little friend.—I am, Sir, &c., E. E. R.

April 27, 1889.

A PARROT'S RECOGNITION OF A LIKE-NESS.

SIR,—I had, a couple of years ago, a king parrot. He used to fly about my study.   On the table I have a letter-weight in the form of a parrot.   The king parrot was constantly in the habit of going through the process of "feeding" the leaden parrot.—I am, Sir, &c.,   W. R. T.

May 11, 1889.

A COCKATOO'S HUMOUR.

SIR,—In confirmation of the statement made in your article upon "Talking Birds," that "cockatoos are almost like monkeys in mimicking men," I beg to send you the following simple story, the truth of which I have every reason to believe, although not personally an eye-witness of the performance. I received the account from a bishop. A very tame sulphur-crested white cockatoo happened to be on his perch near a lawn-tennis ground. The day was damp and the ground slippery. In the course of the game several falls occurred. Each tumble gave rise to much laughter and merriment amongst both players and onlookers, which seemed to attract the especial attention of the bird. When the "set" was finished, and the performers were talking together on one side of the court, "Cocky" quietly descended from his stand, walked on to the lawn-tennis ground, rolled over and over two or three times on the grass, and then picking himself up, laughed long and loud in exact imitation of the players!—I am, Sir, &c.,

W. HILL JAMES, Lieut.-Col.

October 18, 1890.

THE SONG OF THE CANARY.

SIR,—I am obliged to your correspondent, "M. H. T.," for the remarks on the song of the wild canary in the *Spectator* of October 25th, which fully bear out my statement of the difference between the note of the wild bird and the song which it has acquired and transmitted to its posterity in captivity. I am sorry if I have done an injustice to their natural song. Dr. Bolle states that it is much inferior to that of the caged bird; and Wilson, speaking of the American wild canary, says: "Its song is so weak as to appear to proceed from a considerable distance, when perhaps the bird is perched on a tree over your head," though he has "heard some sing in *cages* with great energy and determination."

Your correspondent, however, has misunderstood the point of my article; he says that if I heard the song of the *wild* canaries, I should never again say that *theirs* was a borrowed song. The statement was not that the wild canaries had borrowed a song, but that the domesticated birds had acquired a different one.— I am, Sir, &c.,

THE WRITER OF THE ARTICLE ON
"TALKING BIRDS."

November 8, 1890.

THE CANARY BIRD.

SIR,—One word more on this subject. Having at one time bred canaries for a good many years, and having also spent a winter in Madeira, I never was more surprised than by the statement of the author of your article on " Talking Birds," that the song of the canary is an acquired one. I went to Madeira quite ignorant of the existence there of the wild canary-finch. Two or three days after my arrival, I heard, and afterwards saw, in the garden of the *quinta* where I was staying, what I never for a moment doubted to be an escaped captive, until my hostess informed me to the contrary.

I should say that the song of the canary has varied less in captivity than the plumage, although it has grown louder, and often harsher. An exact reverter to the wild type in both respects sometimes occurs. I have had a cock-bird—the descendant, no doubt, of many generations of captives—which might, I believe, have been turned out in Madeira without any one discovering from either song or plumage that it was not a wild one.—I am, Sir, &c.,   J. M. L.

November 15, 1890.

A TALKING CANARY.

Sir,—Having read your article on "Talking Birds," in the *Spectator* of October 4th, I think you may like to hear of a canary who had been taught to repeat a phrase, and could do it much more sweetly than a parrot. He was not a German bird, nor of any remarkable breed at all, and was bought when very young, chiefly on account of his beauty. His colour was a bright buff, and he had brown velvety marks on his little crest and on his wings, and an alert, bright manner, not at all shy, although he objected to having people put their hands very near him. He had a loud, but not particularly sweet or fine song. His mistress used to talk to him a good deal, and call him "Pretty," and gradually he began to try to answer and repeat the word. So she used to say, "Sweet, pretty boy," over and over to him, with the intention of his learning it, as she had known of one canary who could say, "Pretty, pretty." He learnt to say this first, as it was easiest for him, being like his own warble, and the word "sweet" was easy also, and like the beginning of his bird-song. "Boy" was more difficult, but after a great many repetitions of "Pretty,

pretty," a prolonged and timid "boy" would finally be added, and then the little fellow would burst into an ecstasy of song in delight at his own achievement. He was extremely affectionate and companionable, and if we wished to make him show off and say his little phrase, we had only to leave him alone in one room, and go into another where he could hear us talking but could not see us, and he would begin to repeat his praise of himself in his best manner, and go on until he had coaxed us to praise him in our turn, and come back to him. He lived to the good old age of eleven, and is still very dear to the hearts of all our family.—I am, Sir, &c.,   F. CANARIA.

November 15, 1890.

A POLITE PARROT.

SIR,—A week or two ago we took our little six-year-old daughter to the Crystal Palace, and when in the parrot-house she became very anxious to secure the beautiful yellow crest-feather which had fallen from one of the cockatoos in the large cage. While we were vainly fishing for it with hairpins, an old cockatoo walked across the cage towards us, somewhat hurriedly but with a dignified and obliging air, and, to our intense surprise, took the feather up in his beak and presented it to us! On our accepting it with joy, he also held forth another pretty white feather which lay near. Need I say that he was rewarded to the best of our power with sundry pieces of cake? I confess I should like to know whether our friend acted on the inspiration of the moment, or whether he is known to pass his life in doing these courtesies. —I am, Sir, &c.,   LOUISA CANZIANI.

August 26, 1893.

SPARROWS.

THE VANITY OF SPARROWS.

SIR,—Permit me to ask those bird-loving correspondents of yours, whose letters I have read with great interest in the *Spectator*, whether they have ever noticed the pleasure that sparrows apparently have in contemplating themselves? My daughter writes to me from Bangalore that she is " obliged to cover up" her " looking-glass with a towel, for the sparrows come in, sit on the frame, and tap at themselves, making both glass and dressing-table in a horrid mess. At first the towel kept them away ; but they were always on the watch, and if any one threw back the towel, they would be there in a minute. But now they hold back the towel with one claw, hold themselves on with the other, and peck away at their images."—I am, Sir, &c., F. C.

August 26, 1893.

THE VANITY OF SPARROWS.

SIR,—Your correspondent's story of the self-con-templating sparrows, in your issue of August 26th, reminds me of a canary I possessed in the days of my youth. Whenever he was let out of his cage he always made for the mirror above the fire-place, and would fly up and down before it, pecking at his image in the glass, and singing as he flew upwards and downwards, with his gaze fixed in the glass. I am inclined to think that in his case it was the desire for companionship, and I think it hard to accuse the sparrows of vanity.—I am, Sir, &c.,   R. S.

September 9, 1893.

SPARROWS.

SIR,—Your correspondent, " R. S.," in the *Spectator* of September 9th, and the writer in the *Daily News* who thought my daughter's " self-contemplating sparrows " worthy of notice, may be interested in the sequel of the story, which came to me from Bangalore by the last mail. One morning she came into her room and found that her maid had caught one of the miscreants, and had tied his legs together with soft wool. My daughter says :—

" I demurred to this as cruel (though it did not hurt him, and he was quite quiet), but she implored me to let him stop on the window-sill for an hour or so as a punishment. So we tied a long woollen string to his leg, and let him hop about, hoping to make friends with him ; but as he refused all our overtures, after a short time we let him fly away. He must have gone straight to all his brothers and sisters, for since that day no sparrow has ever appeared in my room, and my looking-glass no longer needs a covering, much to my maid's satisfaction, as before, it was a case of a clean toilet-cover every day."

Trusting this instance of the means of communication possessed by birds may interest some readers.— I am, Sir, &c., F. C.

October 14, 1893.

SPARROWS.

SIR,—Your correspondent, " F. C.," in the *Spectator* of August 26th, refers to the singular fancy which sparrows occasionally betray for admiring themselves in a looking-glass.   During the past summer I have witnessed this on two or three occasions; but the most amusing point was that when a hen-sparrow kept sitting on the edge of the looking-glass, intently admiring and pecking mildly at herself, the cock-bird repeatedly flew down also on to the glass and tried to make her desist, not without lingering for a moment or two to have a look at himself.   Whether the feminine vanity or masculine jealousy was most reprehensible in this case may be a fair ground for dispute between the human sexes.—I am, Sir, &c.,   M.

October 21, 1893.

A STRANGE SPARROW

SIR,—There is a Jenny Wren's nest on a bough of a cedar-tree in this garden. Noticing a female house-sparrow constantly flying towards the nest, my curiosity was aroused, and I decided to watch. To my astonishment I found the sparrow was feeding the young ones; only one wren, so far as I can ascertain, ever visits the nest. Is it possible that the sparrow knows by instinct that one parent is dead, and has therefore taken pity on the ground birds? I should add that on one occasion when the wren approached the nest it found the sparrow inside, and was apparently much distressed, and for some time the sparrow refused to quit. As soon as it did the wren fed its young, and immediately flew away in search of more food.—I am, Sir, &c.,

J. ALEXANDER SMITH.

August 10, 1895.

9

TOMTITS.

TOMTITS.

SIR,—Let me give you the following bit of natural history, called forth by your article in the *Spectator* of February 12th, on the calculating faculty in animals, as illustrated in Sir J. Lubbock's late lecture.

A few years ago, in a park near Ware, in Herts, a small box was hung on a tree near the house, with a small hole at one end, for birds to nest in if they would. Soon a pair of tomtits took possession, and after much busy constructiveness, ten little eggs, and in due time ten little chicks made a family party. Whether he was weary of housekeeping, or fell in with a counter-attraction, or was caught budding a greengage-tree, was never ascertained; but Mr. Tit one day did not return home. Poor Mrs. Tit did her best for some time; but finding not only her own strength failing, but her little fledglings gradually wasting, she thought it better to save her due share of them than lose all. One morning, five of the young ones were found lying dead under the hole of the box, she having ejected them. This would seem

to evidence not merely the faculty of numeration,
but of passing in the first four rules of arithmetic.
Clearly there was division and subtraction ; and the
sense that could conclude that the half of ten is five,
might also be conscious that twice five is ten.—I am,
Sir, &c., M.

February 19, 1887.

THE TOMTIT IN LONDON.

SIR,—The tomtits (both larger and smaller) are by no means unfamiliar in London, but take kindly to any fairly quiet garden where they are treated with kindness. For years I have hung up meat-bones for them to feed on during the severe weather, and they have requited the consideration by a constant exhibition of the most entertaining gymnastics all day long. Two half-cocoanuts were also hung up in an old verandah, which runs round one side of the house, last winter, and were constantly visited by titmice, who cleared them out in a short time. Some hanging flower-baskets, lined with dead moss, were suspended in the same verandah, and in the late summer, the tits, after busily boring holes in the moss as if to make nests, have come regularly every night to roost in them. At dusk they may be seen flitting round the baskets, and, finally tucking themselves into the holes, they sleep there with such confidence that no passing footstep or near voice disturbs them. All this goes on, literally, within a stone's-throw of the four-mile radius. Other birds, such as robins, thrushes, and blackbirds build, in the summer, in the same garden, where they find a regular meal in the winter, showing that they—like dogs and horses—know who are kind to them, and whom they may trust.—I am, Sir, &c., ELLIOT STOCK.

November 7, 1891.

A TOMTIT'S NEST.

Sir,—A pair of tomtits have built and hatched under an inverted flower-pot in my garden. The nest is on the ground, but in a sheltered and very dry position, and the flower-pot is 11 inches in depth with a diameter or base of 13 inches. The tomtit builds a closed nest entered by a small opening at the side, and in this case the adaptation of the habit to the situation is curious. On the removal of the covering flower-pot, a circular cushion filling the whole ground-space is shown, nearly 2 inches in thickness ; moss on the ground, wool and hair above, like the wall of the ordinary nest. The nest proper, with about a dozen young birds, is at one side, where the slope of the pot and a sort of protecting wall or pad of wool would act as a covering ; and the old birds have access through the hole in the bottom of the flower-pot. How the young birds are to get out of this nest, with some 10 inches of vertical flight to manage, is not clear.—I am, Sir, &c.,

F. Simcox Lea.

May 27, 1893.

ANOTHER TOMTIT'S NEST.

SIR,—Singular as it is, I doubt whether Mr. Simcox Lea's nest is so remarkable as one I have here. The striking-post of my entrance-gate consists of an iron column tapering upwards, solid for 20 inches from the base, but hollow thence to the top, with a rectangular opening 6 inches high by 1 inch wide, beginning at 2 feet 2 inches from the base, and used for the admission of the bolt of the gate. The inside diameter of the hollow space within the column is about $2\frac{1}{2}$ inches, with the result that there exists a kind of cup 6 inches deep below the opening, the bottom of which cup is 8 inches or a little more under the bolt when shot. In this cup, for upwards of twenty years past, a pair of tomtits (how often the same pair is unascertainable) has annually nested, and, except in one instance when a cat destroyed the sitting hen, the majority of the young tits have thriven and flown. The bolt is withdrawn and replaced with considerable noise at least thirty to forty times daily, but the parent birds wholly disregard both the motion and the noise. This year and now, we have, so far as they can be counted, seven young tits hatched out and likely to fly within a week ; but how these young birds or their predecessors contrive to reach the opening of escape, I have never been able to discover. Eight years ago the annual addition of wool and hair made to the nest, and the accumulation of bones and *débris* of young birds which had died or failed to escape, had filled the hollow cup to such a point, that there was risk of the bolt injuring the sitting hen, and I therefore cleaned it out ; whereupon, the following year, a pair of tits recommenced from the bottom, and the process of filling it up has again arrived so far that I have this morning been able to insert my finger into the mouths of the fledglings, and must therefore, when they are gone, again clear out the cup.—I am, Sir, &c.,   J. H. JAMES.

June 3, 1893.

TOMTIT ARCHITECTURE.

SIR,—Your correspondent's tomtit nesting letter, in the *Spectator* of May 27th, was most interesting. But the problem in gymnastics to be solved by the young tits is only apparently a difficult one, inasmuch as it has been solved by the parent birds. Your correspondent's conception of the difficulty is the result of his evident forgetfulness of the fact that young birds are not so stupid or so incomplete as young babies. The titmice will get out of the hole of the inverted flower-pot in exactly the same way as their parents do. But in our rectory garden just now we have a still more curious problem in tit architecture. A pair of great-tits have built their nests in the iron chimney of a disused greenhouse-stove. The pipe is perpendicular, of 3 inches diameter, and is about 12 feet long. The nest is constructed about 6 feet down. There are eight young birds, nearly ready to—(?) fly, climb, be carried, washed down—how get out? What will your correspondent suggest?

By the way, why will people speak of *tom*-tits? There are great-tits, blue-tits, cole-tits, longtailed-tits, marsh-tits, crested-tits! But what is a tomtit?—I am, Sir, &c., MAURICE STUBBS.

June 3, 1893.

THE REASONING FACULTY IN BIRDS.

BIRD INTELLIGENCE.

SIR,—In the spring of 1877 my gardener was requested to try to rear a pair of young blackbirds. He fixed on one nest, in some ivy, about thirty yards away from the house. On a certain Sunday morning he saw that the birds were hatched; on the next Sunday he peeped into the nest, and saw the little ones were going on well. On the following Sunday morning he peeped again, and lo! the nest was empty. He was very much surprised, and as he stood by the tree, wondering what had become of the birds, he was attracted to a pair of parent birds in a neighbouring tree. They had food in their mouth, and made a curious noise, as they flew restlessly from one tree to another. Thinking they might be the parents of his lost *protégés*, he decided to watch their movements. They flew away and back again, returning *each time* to rest nearer the house, until one of them flew rapidly across the drive, under the

verandah, and back again, as in a moment. The
other followed immediately in the same way, and
then they both flew off. Seeing this, the man placed
himself in half-hiding, determined to await their
return. In due time they came back, flew fearlessly
to their young, and less hurriedly went away again.
Thus their young were discovered in a hollow over a
projection under the verandah-roof. There cannot
be a doubt that these were the young birds removed
from the nest in the tree to this very safe and very
unlikely place of retreat.

Assuming this, and considering the whole incident
from the point of view of human intelligence, there
is a series of complicate mental acts, which seems to
indicate a very large measure of mind in these two
birds. There must have been suspicion, passing into
conviction, of the intention of the gardener; determination to prevent the robbery contemplated; agree-
ment as to the manner in which this could be accom-
plished; the looking for and choosing the most likely
place for their new home, then choosing the time and
arranging the manner of the removal; and finally,
the mechanical act of carrying their three young ones,
already a fortnight old, from the nest, a distance of
full thirty yards, to their new home.

Is it not justifiable, and in fact necessary, to accept
this analysis as true to the case before us? There
could have been no antecedent experience to dictate
the course pursued. "The logic of feeling" rises in
such a case to the logic of intellect, and though the
processes I have described may have had different

conditions in the limited brain of these feathered intelligences, I cannot help thinking that the processes must have been so similar, as to class this instance of animal intelligence with the same operations as conducted in the higher order of mind.

I may just add, the young ones were never taken. They had a capital run of some yards, and whenever we tried to take them they always ran away, until they flew off their own masters.—I am, Sir, &c.,

J. S.

October 26, 1878.

THE REASON OF BIRDS.

SIR,—In your issue of the 27th ult. you quote a story told in some of the papers of hawks having been noticed, in parts of England and France, to fly after railway-trains in order to pounce on the small birds put up by the trains. You draw certain deductions, "if that story is true," and say that "it needs precise verification." I have myself observed a similar thing happen in India. The East India Railway between the Toondla Junction and Agra runs at one place over a high embankment, the outside slopes of which are planted with the "babool" tree. The tops of these, three years ago, were about on a level with the windows of the carriages, and shook and waved as the train rushed by.

Travelling one day in the same carriage with one of the railway staff, who had occasion to pass over the line very often, he told me, on approaching the spot, to look out for "the hawks chasing the birds." As the tree-tops shook and swayed, the small birds flew out of them, and the hawks which, whether waiting or not, were close by, flew after them. It is, of course, possible that the neighbourhood may have been one favoured of hawks, who, seeing the birds in troubled flight, went after them. But there was no reason to suppose this, the gentleman attached to the railway had observed it as a new thing, and he had no doubt that the hawks came and waited because they knew the tree-tops would shake and the birds rush out.—I am, Sir, &c.,

R. E. FORREST, P.W.D., India.

October 4, 1879.

THE REASON OF BIRDS.

SIR,—May I tell you a few facts, to prove that birds can be, like their human friends, both reasonable and unreasonable? 1. Several years ago a pair of my canaries built; while the hen was sitting, the weather became intensely hot. She drooped, and I began to fear that she would not be strong enough to hatch the eggs. I watched the birds closely, and soon found that the cock was a devoted nurse. He bathed in the fresh cold water I supplied every morning, then went to the edge of the nest, and the hen buried her head in his breast and was refreshed. Without hands and without a sponge, what more could he have done? 2. The following spring the same bird was hanging in a window with three other canaries, each in a separate cage. I was sitting in the room, and heard my little favourite give a peculiar cry. I looked up, and saw all the birds crouching on their perches, paralysed with fright. On going to the window to ascertain the cause of their terror, I saw a large balloon passing over the end of the street. The birds did not move till it was out of sight, when they all gave a chirp of relief. The balloon was only within sight of the bird who gave the alarm, and I have no doubt he mistook it for a bird of prey.   3. I have a green and a yellow canary hanging side by side.   They are treated exactly alike, and are warm friends.   One has often refused to partake of some delicacy till the other was supplied with it.   One day I had five blossoms of dandelion ; I gave three to the green bird, two to the yellow one. The latter flew about his cage, singing in a shrill voice and showed unmistakable signs of anger.   Guessing the cause, I took away one of the three flowers, when both birds settled down quietly to enjoy their feast.— I am, Sir, &c.,   K. H.

October 18, 1879

BIRDS, AND THEIR SUPPOSED POWER OF COUNTING.

SIR,—I read with much interest the article in the *Spectator* of February 12th, on Sir John Lubbock's lecture, and especially the question raised concerning the arithmetical power of animals. As far as birds are concerned, I have always believed that the discovery that eggs have been taken from the nest is not due to any power of counting, but to the much simpler sensation of feeling. My ground for this belief is an experiment I have frequently made upon the common plover. This bird, as is well known, always places its four eggs point to point. The object of this is to enable the mother-bird, which is small in proportion to the size of the eggs, to cover them more completely when sitting. Now, I have found that when I have removed two of the eggs, whether opposite or next to each other, the bird has generally deserted. In the few cases where this has not been the case, the two remaining eggs have been placed by the mother so that the narrow ends overlap considerably. Taking this hint, I have tried the experiment of altering the two remaining eggs to this position myself, and have found that, almost invariably, the nest is not deserted. This makes me think that the immediate cause of desertion is the discomfort arising from the altered shape of the eggs taken together, not any distinct appreciation of number as such ; or perhaps it would be more correct to say, the sense of danger which this feeling of discomfort produces. It is a well-known fact that many birds will desert if a nest is the least disturbed, even without any eggs being taken. Birds have little or no power of distinguishing either the colour or shape of the single eggs, as birds will continue to sit on the eggs of other birds, and even stones, after their own have been taken away. The feeding of a young bird in a cage by its mother surely is best explained by supposing that the mother hears and recognises the cry of its young one. It is hardly necessary to suppose that the mother is the least aware of its absence from the nest until she hears it crying for food. This power of crying is developed long before the bird is well enough fledged to leave the nest.—I am, Sir, &c.,   F. H. WOODS.

February 19, 1887.

FIDELITY IN BIRDS.

SIR,—I think the many bird-lovers who frequent your columns will like to share the following experience with me. I walked over this morning to call on a friend whose wife is a skilful ornithologist, and has the brightest and healthiest aviaries known to me. I was particularly struck with one of them, that for foreign finches, in which some fifty birds from all quarters of the globe were flitting about, and prattling to one another on the swinging perches. They were of all colours, generally very brilliant, and almost all unknown to me. Amongst those that attracted me most was a gentle little hen, almost white, a "zebra finch," the mistress told me, which she had got through an advertisement in *Exchange and Mart* from a perfect stranger. Rather more than a week after the arrival of the "zebra finch," she had another letter from her correspondent, saying that a "Bengalese," who had shared the cage of the "zebra finch," had shown such evident signs of distress ever since their separation that if she would put 2s. 6d. into the poor-box, and accept the disconsolate bird, he should be sent off at once. She gladly complied with the condition, and

in due course the " Bengalese " arrived, and was turned
into the finch aviary.   Here, amongst the fifty strangers,
he at once singled out his lost love, who was sitting
meekly on a perch in a distant corner, and flew straight
up to her side.   She seemed equally delighted, and
they rubbed bills and shoulders, and in the intervals
of such birdlike caressings prattled away to each other
as though recounting their respective adventures since
that sad parting ten days before.   To-day there was
not a brighter bird in the aviary than that " Bengalese,"
or one more unlike his faithful mate in plumage or
form.—I am, Sir, &c.,   THOMAS HUGHES.

P.S.—The cuckoo was heard here for the first time
this morning ; a cheery greeting for the holiday-folk

April 27, 1889.

THE AFFECTION OF BIRDS.

SIR,—Dr. Kay, commenting on Psalm civ. 17, tells a story about the stork similar to that published in the *Spectator* of July 5th. He says that the name *Chasidah* is equivalent to *pia avis*, and suggests that "stork" may be cognate with στοργή.

The parental affection of the eagle was sufficiently known among the Israelites to serve as an illustration of the protecting guidance of God. "As an eagle stirreth up her nest, fluttereth over her young, spreadeth abroad her wings, taketh them, beareth them on her wings : so the Lord alone did lead him." In the New Testament our Lord illustrated the divine solicitude in a similar way : "How often would I have gathered thy children together, even as a hen gathereth her chickens under her wings."

The power which has been given to birds of returning love other than parental, may be illustrated from numerous sources. St. Francis wooed and won their love : "The redbreasts picked up crumbs on his table, the pheasant nestled at his side, the falcon woke him to prayer, and the swallow hovered round his bedside and sang him to sleep when his last hour came." St

Hugh, at the Great Chartreuse, "tamed the little birds
. . . to such an extent that they would leave their
woods, and regularly at the hour of supper would come
to share his meal with him, not only getting on his
table, but eating out of his hand and his plate, and
making themselves completely his companions." At
Witham, "a certain little bird which is called 'Burneta'
came every day to his table, as though it had discovered
the innate kindness of the man, and took its food from
his hand and his plate." In Lincolnshire he was faithfully loved, equally when present and when absent, by
his beautiful swan. In "England under the Angevin
Kings," I., 77–79, an account is given of St. Godric,
who said: "He who denies himself the converse of
men wins the converse of birds and beasts, and the
company of angels." St. Cuthbert won such love from
the eider-ducks that they nestled in his lap, and he
loved them so that eider-ducks were embroidered on
his dalmatic. St. Guthlac, too, "was in league with
the fowls of the air; the wild birds . . . would eat
from his hand; swallows came to sit on his arms and
his bosom;" and he said: "He who is joined to God
with a pure spirit finds all things uniting themselves
to him in God."—I am, Sir, &c.,

ROBERT G. FOOKES.

July 19, 1890.

\

MEMORY OF BIRDS.

SIR,—Last year I fed the tomtits with a cocoanut suspended on a stick outside my window, and they came greedily. This year I forgot all about it, but hearing a clamour in a fuchsia-bush outside my study-window during the snow of last week, I found myself besieged by an army of tomtits, who had taken this effectual means of reminding me of my want of care. Was it memory, or association of ideas, or both?—I am, Sir, &c.,   F. G. MONTAGU POWELL.

December 6, 1890.

MEMORY OF BIRDS.

SIR,—Your readers may be interested by the following incident displaying the wonderful power of memory which some birds possess. Some time ago we had a cock of the black, single-comb Spanish breed. The farm-boy, who lived about five hundred yards from the farm, was in the habit of encouraging this cock to spur at him, so that every morning, as he went to his work, a pugilistic encounter took place between boy and cock. After a time the boy left us and went to London. Returning at the end of six months, he paid a visit to his fellow-labourers at the farm. He was immediately recognised by the cock, and on coming out of his cottage the next morning he found the bird waiting outside for him ready again to face his opponent. This continued for several days, until one afternoon the boy came to the farm to wish his companions good-bye, as he was returning to London ; and the next morning the cock omitted to pay his usual visit. We thus have an instance of the memory of a bird stretching over the space of six months.—I am, Sir, &c.,

FLORENCE BARFORD.

December 13, 1890.

BIRDS AND LANGUAGE.

BIRD LANGUAGE.

SIR,—I have read with much interest the article on
" The Language of Animals " which appeared in your
issue of April 7th. From it I gather that although
no one can understand the talk of beasts and birds
so as to be able to converse with them and establish
a communication of thought, yet it is possible from
frequent observations of the behaviour of animals
when emitting certain sounds, to arrive approxi-
mately at the meaning of such sounds. Now, I have
some knowledge of the behaviour of small caged
birds, especially of bullfinches, and after reading your
article I feel somewhat puzzled to account for the
uniform behaviour of various bullfinches under certain
circumstances which I wish here to detail. Bullfinches frequently emit a peculiar grating, hissing
noise, accompanied by flapping of the wings and
ruffling up of the feathers, all of which signs would
certainly betoken anger, and I have every reason to
believe *do* betoken anger, when used against other

birds, because under such circumstances, provided they can reach each other, a severe battle ensues. I have called this noise swearing. Now, there is no question of the fondness of my bullfinches for me, for I have possessed some that I could set free in the garden and call back to my hand at will ; and yet I find that they frequently make this same noise at me, accompanying it by the same actions of menace. I cannot think that the noise then expresses dislike of me, for it is to me that any luxuries or joys of their present caged condition are due. Can it be possible that they use the same noise to me to betoken an entirely different sentiment from that which they feel when they utter it against their own kind ? Thinking this may interest those of your readers who have given any thought to the subject of the " language of animals," I am writing this to you, Mr. Editor, trusting at the same time that some one who has had experience in such matters may be able to offer a satisfactory explanation.—I am, Sir, &c.,

C. S. COBB.

April 21, 1888.

THE LANGUAGE OF BIRDS.

SIR,—Mock anger seems to be rather common among birds. There is in them, when caged, some suppressed excitement, or fury, especially in the spring. Every one who knows a parrot, knows that a perfectly reciprocal fondness is no protection against his bite. The one I know bites his best friend deeply, and roars with laughter. The little birds use a kind of flirtation of defiance with the overwhelming power of those they know intimately. A skilled bird-tamer, I believe, puts his hand into the cage, and when the bird moves, withdraws it hurriedly, as if in fear. This invites the bird to a contempt which becomes the foundation for familiarity; and the device is founded, I suppose, on that adventurous and provocative spirit in the bird which prompted the bullfinches to scold and bully the master whose favours they value. Does a puppy bark and snap in play in something like the same temper?

I might mention a goldfinch I know, which, I think, never fails to distinguish its partial mistress from all others by an outburst of swearing and ruffling.—I am, Sir, &c., P. N. WAGGETT.

April 28, 1888.

THE LANGUAGE OF BIRDS.

SIR,—I have no hesitation in saying that when bull-finches gape, hiss, and flutter their wings to those they like, as mentioned by Mr. Cobb, they do so as expressive of affection or thanks, and not at all as "swearing." I have often been amused at this characteristic from a long acquaintance with them. As I approach them with a tit-bit, they thus salute me, and take it from my hand with kisses. It is true they go through the same performance when enraged, except the kissing ; but there is nothing at all unusual in all this, if we remember that the play of most animals is a close imitation of their challenge and combat. In spite of its apparent identity, I can hear the temper of the bullfinch in its voice, just as easily as I can tell whether my dog be vexed or pleased by his bark ; yet these differences are not distinguishable by a strange ear. These differences in tone are well understood by the respective species and we learn to understand them from familiarity with individuals. If it be true that a musician can strike a given note on a piano with a score of different expressions, surely a bird's eloquence is not less limited.

If play be generally mimic war, may not all kissing (including that of animals) be the "survival" of biting?—I am, Sir, &c., E. W. PHIBBS.

April 28, 1888.

COURTESY AND DISCOURTESY IN BIRDS.

COCKS AND HENS.

SIR —We are all familiar with the delightful gallantry with which a barn-door cock will, on finding food, call his hens, and point out the food, and bow and scrape while they eat it. I witnessed, however, the other day, an act of such perfect courtesy on the part of two little birds, that I think you will be glad to record it. We have a large cage in which are a number of various birds, among them a cock gold-finch and two little mannikins. These latter little sober-coloured birds we considered very uninterest-ing. Wishing, however, to provide a mate for the goldfinch, I one evening bought a hen canary, and the next morning turned it into the cage with the others. None of the other birds took the least notice of the new arrival, but the two little mannikins placed themselves side by side by the seed-vessel, and, the canary being on a perch above, they fed her in turn with seed, lifting up their little black heads, one after the other, and letting her take the seed out of their stumpy white beaks. This appeared to be pure courtesy to the lady stranger. We have seen no repetition of the act ; but, one of the mannikins having got wet one day, we watched the canary returning the courtesy by trying to dry its feathers by passing them through her beak.—I am, Sir, &c.,

WM. WALSHAM BEDFORD,
Bishop Suffragan for East London.

April 19, 1884.

REFINEMENT IN BIRDS.

SIR,—What my friend the Bishop of Bedford calls "the delightful gallantry" of the barn-door cock towards his hens is too familiar to warrant particular attention. If I were to tell of the care with which on one occasion I saw the "paterfamilia" of my own poultry-yard break the shells of a basketful of snails and present the unctuous morsels one by one to his wives, with the utmost courtesy, I should be only mentioning what the observation of others could easily parallel.

The following instance of the same refined attention is, however, I think, sufficiently unusual to deserve record. When I was a boy there were two farmyards attached to my father's house—one near, the other more distant. The fowls had not thriven very well in the near farmyard, and it was thought better to remove them to the other. This was done at night, after the cock and his seraglio had gone to roost. The next day we boys, anxious to know how the fowls were getting on in their new quarters, accompanied our father to the place to which they had been removed. The hens were busily scratching on the dunghill, as happy as ever, but the cock was nowhere to be seen. On asking the farming-man where he was, he opened the hen-house door with a queer grin, and there we saw our old friend busily employed in making nests for his hens to lay in. Though more than half a century has passed, I can see him now in the dusky background of the shed, actively arranging the straw with his feet, and re-monstrating against our intrusion on his pious work by a surprised and querulous chuckle. I hope his numerous wives were properly grateful for this self-sacrificing labour.—I am, Sir, &c.,

EDMUND VENABLES.

April 26, 1884.

COURTESY IN BIRDS.—THE DUCK.

SIR,—The two illustrations of courtesy in birds given by your correspondent in the *Spectator* of April 19th are attractive and interesting. Every observer of the habits of our domestic fowls must be familiar with the gallantry of the barn-door cock, who, when he discovers a dainty morsel, summons his harem to the banquet, and stands aloof while the ladies eat, not tasting himself. It is well that there should be a redeeming feature in the character of that fire-eating, pompous, and tyrannical creature. I think he possesses no other respectable trait, except perhaps his undoubted courage, which continues until he has been once well thrashed, when as a rule he becomes a wretched craven. I regret to say that I have known more than one barn-door cock, who, without having discovered any food at all, would pretend to have done so, and when some hen, responding to his call, had come within his reach, would conduct himself in a very ungentlemanly way towards her.

Now the duck is considered a particularly uninteresting and prosaic animal. Yet I venture to affirm that, in point of intelligence, social kindness, and sagacity, he is vastly superior to the barn-door or any other cock or hen. I have kept and closely watched hundreds of ducks ; I never saw them fight with each other, nor ever knew a duck the aggressor in a dispute with some other kind of fowl. But I have witnessed striking instances of charity and kindness in ducks. Let one such case suffice. Amongst some fifty or sixty head of ducks and fowls, I once had a solitary little old bantam hen. She became blind, or nearly so, and like other birds in that condition, " sulked " as it is called, *i.e.*, kept by herself in a dark, retired corner of the fowl-house, knowing instinctively that her cruel and cowardly brethren and sisters would persecute her to death if she appeared amongst them. Here she might, perhaps, have starved, but for the constant and sympathetic attentions of a duck. Twice daily, every day so long as the poor bantam lived, some three weeks, this good Samaritan in the form of a duck was observed to fill her capacious beak with from twenty to thirty grains of barley, with which she proceeded to the fowl-house, and there deposited her store immediately in front of the bantam. Several members of my family, as well as myself, were frequent witnesses of this beautiful incident.

One more anecdote in evidence of the sagacity of the duck. I had five Aylesbury ducks, with a number of fowls. The lord of the yard, a most despotic chanticleer, would never suffer the ducks to feed with his family and friends when, at the regular meal-times, the grain was scattered for their common use.

Ferociously and without pity he drove them from the ground. This had been going on for many weeks, and one day at the 12 o'clock repast, the act of expulsion was performed as usual. I was present, and saw the discomfited ducks retire to a corner of the yard. There they evidently held a conference. Having been so engaged some five minutes, they proceeded with deliberate and resolute air, in single file, as is their wont, towards their oppressor. Having reached the tyrant, they surrounded him, each duck turning his posteriors towards the enemy, and with concerted action fairly hustled him clean out of the yard. To see the surprise of the cock as he jumped from side to side to avoid the pressure of the attacking party, was ludicrous in the extreme. The victory was complete ; from that hour the ducks were never again molested.

I suspect the general notion of the stupidity of the duck arises from his awkward waddling motion as he progresses over the ground. He is not in his natural element on the dry earth. He navigates the water with rapidity, dignity, and grace. In his wild state he is a perfect artist in aerial locomotion. Observe the fine, acute angle described by a flock of wild ducks in their rapid flight ; with what perfect regularity they break-up and re-form when they change the direction of their route ! And if "quack, quack !" is not a musical sound, the weird whir of a company of ducks piercing through space certainly is. Finally, it is urged against the duck that he eats filth. How little reason is there in this reproach ! Dirt is defined to be matter in the wrong place, but the refuse which the duck enjoys, and which he transforms into the most delicious food that issues from the poultry-yard, is anything rather than matter in the wrong place, and is not therefore, in the case of the duck, dirt.— I am, Sir, &c., SIDNEY M. HAWKES.

May 10, 1884.

DISCOURTESY IN BIRDS.

SIR,—A day or two ago I saw the reverse of the picture as I was walking in Kensington Gardens. A duck had not long hatched out a brood of eleven ducklings, which were swimming on the Long Water. One of the bystanders threw some crumbs of bread to the young ones, upon which the duck savagely attacked one or two of the unoffending ducklings, seized them in her bill, and ducked them for several seconds under the water, or rather held them under the water till she was obliged to come up to the surface to breathe, otherwise she must inevitably have drowned them. I can only conclude that she must have been hungry to have ill-treated them in so unnatural a way.—I am, Sir, &c.,   C. R. T.

P.S.—This " duck " reminds me of (and must surely be some distant connection of) the bird I saw down in a " bill of fare " at a restaurant in Paris, with this English translation annexed—viz., " Canard sauvage [trans.], *savage* duck " !

May 17, 1884.

ÆSTHETIC BIRDS.

VAIN SPARROWS.

SIR,—In connection with the article in the *Spectator* of May 2nd, giving examples of the love of beauty by animals, your readers may be interested in the following case of vanity—shall we call it?—lately told us by a missionary friend of ours. She, with her husband, was stationed at Negapatam, where the ubiquitous sparrow would appear to be more ubiquitous than usual. Anyhow, Mrs. L—— was much bothered by the birds coming in to look at themselves in the looking-glass in her dressing-room, till at last she covered the glass with a towel. But the birds were not to be beaten. One day, on entering the room, she caught them at it again, one of the pair holding back a corner of the towel, while the other—and, alas for the credit of our sex! I have to confess that it was the cock-bird—was viewing his beauties in the glass.—I am, Sir, &c.

PHILIP THOMPSON.

July 4, 1891.

ANIMAL ÆSTHETICS.

SIR,—The writer of the admirable article on "Animal Æsthetics," which was published in your columns on May 2nd last, will, I am sure, be interested to learn that a pair of goldfinches in my garden have acted in a manner precisely similar to that practised by the birds of which he wrote. They have built high up in an ilex-tree, and have put the finishing touches to their work by ornamenting the nest with sprigs of the blue forget-me-not. Let us hope that in this case the æsthetic taste of the birds will not, as in the instance quoted in the article referred to, lead to the ruin of their nest.—I am, Sir, &c.,

T. M. WARD (Colonel).

July 11, 1891.

A MUSICAL WOOD-PIGEON.

Sir,—You may like to add the following to Dr. Littledale's story of the musical cat. One day, during the severest part of last winter, a poor starved wood-pigeon was driven to find shelter in Sir Arthur Hazlerigg's house at Noseley. It was fed and cared for, and was so well pleased with its new quarters that it seems wholly to have forgotten its wild nature. It now lives contentedly in a large cage in one of the rooms, with two doves for its companions, flies about the room when let out, and allows itself to be caught and fondled. But the most curious feature of its domesticated life is that when Miss Hazlerigg goes to the piano, the bird will perch on her head or shoulders, and hop about the piano ; but if any other person plays, it will take no notice. Where did it get that discriminating power ?—I am, Sir, &c.,

CHARLES H. NEWMARCH.

September 17, 1881.

MISCELLANEOUS.

MEN AND BIRDS—AN AUTHENTIC TALE.

SIR,—Some little time ago I read with pleasure in the columns of the *Times* a letter from the pen of Mr. Morris, affording interesting information on the affection and social habits of birds—such as the kingfisher, the golden-crested wren, and the wood-pigeon. I, too, have a tale to tell of the sparrow, which, perhaps, you will favour me by inserting in your valuable paper, as an additional evidence of the instinct and attachment of birds. My sparrow's love continued unbroken for years, and this is the unvarnished history of the little affectionate creature.

The rectory of Christ Church, in the island of Barbabos, West Indies, where I resided, is prettily situated amidst trees on a hill overlooking a fishing village, where the waters of the sea, on a clear summer day, are of all colours of green, and where the tropical heat is softened down by a constant land breeze. This is just the abode suited to birds, and consequently the neighbourhood abounds in sparrows. Being alone at the time, many of the sparrows soon

struck up an acquaintance with me, and were among
the first to make their appearance in the most un-
ceremonious manner at the breakfast-table. One of
them, however, more familiar than the rest, seemed
determined that I should adopt it as a pet. By
degrees I induced it to pick bread-crumbs out of my
hand. Our acquaintance gradually matured into un-
suspecting friendship, and ended at last in positive
love, as the sequel will show.

Lengthened time rolled on, and every day the
sparrow was my constant companion. If I was in my
study, it was there. If I was reading in the drawing-
room, it was perched on the tip of my boot. If I did
not rise by daylight, it would come in at the window,
left open purposely for its convenience, and flutter
upon my body, begging, as it were, that I would
attend to its early wants. And more than this. I
missed the bird for a while, and grieved, thinking that
it had fallen a prey to some voracious cat or to the
gunshot of some wayfaring traveller. Every day I
went to the accustomed window and called it by
name (for I had given it the name of "Dick"), but
no Dick appeared. I persevered, however, in loudly
calling for it, as it knew my voice well ; and after an
absence of some weeks, I one morning observed *three*
sparrows flying directly towards me. I held out my
hand as usual, and they alighted on the palm of it.
To my agreeable surprise, there was Mr. or Mrs. Dick
(I know not which), with two well-fledged olive-
branches, which were handed over to me for adoption.
This is not all. Mrs. Dick—for from her affection I

shall assume it was the mother-bird—resolved to build her nest another time nearer home, and repeatedly came to me with a straw in her beak, evidently hoping that I would be her assistant-architect. Finding that I declined the task, she selected a rose-tree, which I could easily touch from my bedroom window, and there entwining three of the tallest branches, she built (as birds only can build) a beautiful nest. From this time she continued to commit her fledglings, as a matter of course, to my care.

But here comes the climax. The time drew near for me to leave the West and to join my family in England, where I am now. It seemed as if my sparrow, by instinct, amounting almost to reason, suspected my movements. Perhaps there was something lonely and strange in the appearance of the rectory, the greater portion of the furniture having been removed ; but be it what it may, Mrs. Dick, although she lived unfettered in the trees, and had the range of the atmosphere, would scarce quit my presence, and, *mirabile dictu*, on returning home one moonlight night, I found the loving bird sleeping like a peaceful infant on my pillow. I could scarce believe my own eyes, but so it was. On approaching to see if it was really a sparrow, it flew upon the top of the wardrobe, and there it remained all the night.

The character of Mrs. Dick was well known, and numerous visitors (among whom I may mention the name of Bishop Mitchinson) often witnessed the influence I had over the sparrow tribe, especially over the one that appeared to sorrow most of all at my departure. I won them by gentleness and kindness, and my reward was ample.

What a moral for man ! What an example for the cultivation of domestic love and affection do we find in these tiny creatures of the feathered race, not one of which falls to the ground without the knowledge of our Heavenly Father! It is time, however, to draw my narrative to a close, and wondering if my petted sparrow is yet alive, I am, Sir, &c.,

F. B. GRANT.

January 1, 1876.

A BARN-YARD INCIDENT.

SIR,—In our earliest brood of chickens last spring was one which grew up to be a bird of singular beauty. He was pure white, and from his stately dignity and general consciousness of his position, the children gave him the name of " Jupiter." He was recognised as an established authority by the sovereign power, and no one disputed his claims ; least of all a bird his junior by a few weeks, which grew up with him, a parti-coloured fowl, of no recognised position in the community of poultry, living in a sort of contempt, or at best of toleration—not even allowed a name by the children, but described by them when necessary in negatives, whom, then, I must call " Outis."

" Jupiter," as the year and his powers advanced, began to treat " Outis " with the greatest indignity and contumely, which " Outis " bore with a quiet patience that perplexed me, as I began to notice his growing strength.   But he dwelt apart, and never crowed ; " Jupiter " being particularly fond of crowing, and usually mounting a hurdle close to the drive for the purpose of exhibiting with greater effect.

At length, in the autumn, matters came to a crisis. There is a thick, dark fir-tree in the field assigned to the poultry, which, generations before any of the existing community were hatched, had been adopted as an universal roosting-place. One evening, after an increasing series of general snubbings and insults, " Jupiter " thought proper to dispute the entrance of the nameless bird into the tree. Half an hour later, exhausted, covered with mud, and utterly forlorn, he, was found lying on the ground beneath the tree, with " Outis " in undisputed possession above. The defeat had been sudden, and it was complete. " Jupiter " has at last recovered the beauty of his plumage, but he lives alone, in worse exile than did his former rival. He has never crowed since his defeat, except —and I fear your readers, who know the beautiful old tradition, will hardly believe the exception, which is true all the same—at sunset on Christmas Eve. " Outis," in his place, crows constantly and loud ; but I am often sorry to see him use his now acknowledged superiority in a very revengeful spirit, as if he remembered past days of his own suffering. On these occasions " Jupiter " is wont to appeal to the State for protection, and he invariably receives it from the sovereign authority, an exceedingly powerful old bird, who settles matters, whenever he takes the trouble, in a very summary way.

We are all very sorry for " Jupiter," whose general grace and culture naturally place him far above his rival, a bird of a somewhat vulgar and commonplace type, though physically strong. But he brought his discomfiture on himself entirely by his own ὕβρις of intolerant self-assertion.

If what I have written reads like an allegory, I cannot help it ; it is literal fact.—I am, Sir, &c.,

F. S. L.

January 8, 1876.

JACKDAWS AND MEN.

SIR,—The following statement, the accuracy of which I can guarantee, may perhaps interest some of your readers. On Saturday last one of my children purchased two young jackdaws from a boy, who probably had taken them from their nest. Jackdaws abound in this island. The young birds were fully fledged, but were scarcely able to fly. They were left for the night on a balcony, in the belief that they could not escape. Early on Sunday morning two old jackdaws made their appearance, and after some trouble succeeded in taking the young birds on their back, and then began to fly away with them. Unfortunately the old birds were startled by the barking of our dogs, and in their panic the little birds fell to the ground. The servants, who witnessed this attempt at rescue, picked up the young birds, and put them into a place of security. One of the birds was apparently injured by its fall, and died a few hours afterwards. Later in the day, as I was sitting in the garden, I saw eight jackdaws circling in the air, and uttering loud cries. Seeing this, I brought the surviving youngling out from its cage, and turned it loose into the garden. I then made every human being quit the garden, and ordered a strict watch to be kept from the house. In a short time the eight jackdaws descended, and called the little one to them. It made a feeble effort to fly, but could only succeed in reaching the lowermost bough of a small tree. Then one of the old jackdaws, coming to it, induced it to mount on him, and then the whole party went off in triumph. This was witnessed by several persons. I do not think that the jackdaws' nest can have been near to my house, which is surrounded by other houses, and has no large trees or rocks in its immediate vicinity.

How did the bereaved old birds find out where their young ones were? How, when they had failed in their first attempt at rescue, did they manage to call in the assistance of friends? I am induced to believe with Cowper, that jackdaws are wiser than men. If, during the Berlin Congress, Lord Cairns and Lord Cranbrook, with the rest of the Cabinet, had flown to Berlin and brought home those two callow fledglings, Lords Beaconsfield and Salisbury, on their backs, the fate of the East might have been changed. I should like to have seen their homeward procession, and would gladly have lent the Ministerial jackdaws some plumes for their triumphant return.— I am, Sir, &c.   FRANK IVES SCUDAMORE.

P.S.—One of my sons declares that the young birds which my little girl purchased were young crows, and not young jackdaws. I think that he is wrong, for I have been well acquainted with crows and jackdaws for many years, but as I do not wish to do any dishonour to the ancient family of my old friend "maître Corbeau," I give my son's view for what it is worth. So far as the instinct and the intelligence of the birds are concerned, it matters little whether they were jackdaws or crows. Politically, I should not be much troubled if the Berlin Congress had been terminated either by the Conservative jackdaws or by the Liberal crows.

July 5, 1879.

STARLINGS NOT FRUIT-EATERS.

SIR,—I am thunderstruck at a most confident assertion in an article upon "Starlings" in *Chambers's
Journal* of this month,—namely, that they are not
fruit-eaters.   The writer professes to have a most
intimate acquaintance with these birds,— watching
their habits day by day at that season of the year
when they return to an old haunt to breed and rear
their young.   I also have for years been intimate
with the starling, and my friendship—if it may be so
called—is not during a particular season, but is an
all-the-year-round one, as it stays with me during the
winter (the writer of the article in question dates from
Scotland, whence the starlings depart in autumn).
Alas for my cherry and mulberry trees,—my cherry-
trees especially!   Fond as I am of these birds, who
dwell with me in scores on the eaves and by the
chimneys, I should have rejoiced exceedingly if they
had *not* been fruit-eaters ; then perhaps there might
have been a chance of a cherry-pie or two—out of
those rosy Kentish cherries—every June.   But no ;
my starlings, for they are my friends in the main, not

only like cherries, but are so fastidious about them
that for one they eat, three or four at least they spoil ;
they must be ripe ; they will, to be sure, take off the
red bite off one side, but the pale half is rejected.
Our paddock in the time of cherries was strewn with
discarded *débris.* Once, making a desperate attempt
to have some of these ripe ones for ourselves, myself
and handmaiden had almost to contend for the spoil
with these marauders. They occupied the top
branches, which were laden with the best, whilst we
gathered from the lower. We waved sticks at them.
" Tcha-a ! " they called out, as much as to say, " We
won't go empty-billed." Nor did they ; we saw each
of them fly off with its bunch, full half of which was
ultimately thrown away. Considering that these
cherry-trees attracted starlings in crowds, we had them
removed and replaced with apple-trees.

Near the house is a fine mulberry-tree. The window
at which I am now writing is on a level with the fruit-
bearing branches. It is also only a few feet below
the starlings' abode. Here, through the spring, looking up from my book or paper, I see with pleasure all
their family and household ways. To this mulberry-
tree the young ones first take their flight from the
nest. A few weeks since, day after day, I counted
fourteen starlings feasting off mulberries. They did
not fly away with them ; they perched on the boughs,
and, half-hidden by the clustering leaves, they ate the
luscious fruit undisturbed. The ground beneath was
stained purple with the quantities they let fall. They
were in the most amusing state of jollity whilst the

mulberry harvest lasted.   For a change of diet they
would sometimes condescend to adjourn to the elder-
berries, but that was only a whim.   How about
starlings not being fruit-eaters?—I am, Sir, &c.,

(MRS.) E. M. EDMONDS.

October 22, 1887.

THE SONGS OF BIRDS AND THE PHONOGRAPH.

SIR,—I was standing for some time a few evenings ago listening to the song of the thrush, which I have listened to a hundred times before with the same feeling with which I wrote in my " History of British Birds ":—" As for the note, that man can have no music in his soul who does not love the song of the throstle." But I noticed at the time, what, indeed, I had often noticed in former years, that while the likeness is general in the song of each and every bird at all times, yet that it varies in this or that one, as in the variations of this or that tune—a general resemblance, a specific difference—no two perhaps ever exactly the same in every note and quaver and trill. It is just the same with the attitudes of birds. Often I have had to say to myself as I looked at a bird in one or other position as it stood perched on a branch or on the ground, that if its likeness had been taken there and then by some exact limner, every one who saw it would have said at once that he knew nothing of birds or of drawing, for that no bird ever naturally stood in any such posture.

But, *a capo*, to the note. No one who in reading for honours at Oxford has taken up Aristophanes for one of his books, will ever be able to forget that most entertaining writer in the accounts of his "Birds." Every one who has read the play will remember what the various birds have said, and how they said it. But neither Aristophanes himself, nor any other writer of verse or prose, could ever reproduce their notes, whether in writing or description, with any exactitude. You listen, and try to keep them in your mind, but it is a vain attempt. You endeavour to imprint each change on your memory, but as vainly : *abiit, evasit, erupit.* There have been numberless attempts to write down in words the notes of the songs of birds, but no one can say that they have been very successful.

But the reason why I have written at such length,, is as a prelude to a thought that occurred to me as I stood listening to the bird I have spoken of. At the moment it occurred to me that it might be quite possible to take down every note of its song by means of the phonograph, and then, by reproducing them more at leisure, they could be written down "in score" by any musician ; Art and Nature thus going hand-in-hand. I may be wrong, but that is what occurred to me as a "happy thought" while I listened to those liquid notes of the song-thrush on the bough overhead.

And, further, I thought what a solace it might be to some sufferer in a sick-room, to be able to enjoy the pleasure without the sad drawback of its being at the cost of some poor bird in a cage.—I am, Sir, &c.,

F. O. MORRIS.

May 31, 1890.

BIRDS IN FOG.

SIR,—With reference to the remark in your interesting article on the above subject in the *Spectator* of December 27th, that "rooks and partridges do not seem to alter their habits in the fog so much as other birds that seek their living in the open country," you may think the following incident worth recording :—Some thirteen or fourteen years ago I was staying in an old house in the suburbs of London, the garden of which, although it was not more than five miles from Hyde Park Corner, was the home of multitudinous birds. One afternoon, during a dense fog that turned day into night, a flight of rooks came over the garden, cawing noisily. They seemed to be wheeling about just overhead discussing the advisability of staying there, and after a few circuits descended into a cedar-tree of great size and beauty which stood close to the house, and after much talk there settled down for the night. There were many and far higher trees all round that one would have thought would have been more likely to show through the fog; possibly the thick foliage and the roomy branches of the cedar that enabled them to roost close together for mutual protection may have influenced their decision in the unusual circumstances in which they found themselves. The next morning, the fog having cleared off, the birds took their departure at daybreak. They had evidently lost their way hopelessly, though they were probably close to home, for though there was no rookery in this particular garden, there was more than one in the immediate neighbourhood, and a large colony within three miles.—I am, Sir, &c.,

H. F. B.

January 10, 1891.

THE LIBELS ON BIRDS.

SIR,—The article in the *Spectator* of February 14th upon " The Sinfulness of Novelty" contained for me one paragraph of special interest, for it was to the effect that "the crow that develops white feathers, and is pecked to death by its fellow-crows, may, for all we know, have excited their jealous anger more than their fear of an unknown monstrosity." Now, I hope it is a fiction that crows peck their fellow-crows to death, from any motive, when they happen to appear in unorthodox colours ; for " Jacko," my tame rook, has lately developed half a dozen white feathers, and rooks and crows so evidently belong to the same family, that how could poor " Jacko " be safe with the " rookery rooks," among whom he spends his days, if their envy or fear was excited by his somewhat variegated appearance?   But they walk and fly about together just as usual, the wild rooks taking not the least notice of " Jacko's " fast-whitening wings.   And from that other libel upon my feathered friends, that if a poor tame bird escapes from its cage, the wild birds will quickly kill it, my own experience would seem to clear them ; for between four and five years ago a beautiful canary suddenly appeared in the garden here—no one ever knew where it came from— and for a whole month it was flying about with the sparrows, who never for a moment seemed to think of harming in any way their yellow-coated little companion. Indeed, if there was any difference, it was "Tweet"—so named because of its pleasant little chirp—that had rather the upper hand; but they were the best possible friends, and were constantly together. Sometimes I should miss him for several hours, and think he was gone altogether; but later in the day he has come back with quite a little flock of sparrows, having evidently shared their flight about the neighbouring gardens. That it did not go away altogether, was perhaps owing to the fact of the constant and liberal supply of canary-seed it found scattered about the gardens, and at last I thought it might be coaxed into the greenhouse by the same means—and it was — and venturing in there one morning for its breakfast, it was easily captured and caged ; and though it had been " on the spree " for so long, and such a "spree" for such a little creature, it was just as happy in captivity as when flying about the trees ; and how glad I was to know it safe from all dangers, from neighbours' cats I had more than once caught watching it, and from the coming winter and almost certain starvation. It was late in September when its adventures were finished, and there were a few quite stormy nights, when I wondered where poor, brave little "Tweet" was roosting.

Now, as this one little tame bird when it flew out

into the world found friends instead of enemies, and as " Jacko " flaunts his white feathers unmolested by his companions, may we not hope that birds are libelled by the general belief that they will "peck to death " a fellow-bird because of anything unusual, either in its "ways" or its appearance?—I am, Sir, &c., S. W.

February 21, 1891.

THE LIBELS ON BIRDS.

SIR,—For a "last word" on the subject of birds pecking their fellow-birds to death merely because of their exhibiting unusual plumage, I should like to suggest that your correspondent, Mr. G. A. Craig, proves rather the cruelty of those on board his vessel than the cruelty of the birds. For where is the analogy between the birds that, from natural causes, have developed white feathers, and the birds that, for a most unnatural "amusement," have been smothered with soot? A love of cleanliness, rather than a dislike of black feathers, may have accounted for the vigorous measures resorted to by the companions of those poor, ill-treated sea-birds. Or, possibly, birds, like many other things, are imitative; and, while the rooks and the sparrows here never meet with anything but kindness, the poor sea-birds that followed (so mistakenly) Mr. Craig's vessel were first caught with fish-hooks that their wings might disfigure bonnets and hats, and to vary the "amusement," those that were not destined for "trimming" were "covered with soot," and then turned loose amongst their frightened and unrecognising companions! Quite possibly, if I were to whitewash poor " Jacko," then turn him loose among the " Rookery rooks," they would not be so untroubled at his appearance as they are at the white feathers of Nature's painting.—I am, Sir, &c.,

S. W.

[The " love of cleanliness " could hardly necessitate the pecking of the blackened bird to death. Our correspondent is not at all too hard on the cruelty of the sailors, but we do not think that he makes out a very good case for his birds.—ED. *Spectator.*]

March 7, 1891.

BIRDS IN LONDON.

SIR,—At Highbury we consider we are in London, and therefore our surprise is great to find the great titmouse (a pair) a frequenter of our garden. We have lived here for many years, but never saw this bird till now. We have always had the robin, thrush, and blackbird. I send this in case you think it worthy of mention in your valuable paper.—I am, Sir, &c.,

A. GARRETT.

October 24, 1891.

BIRDS IN LONDON.

SIR,—Having read the interesting accounts of unusual bird-visitors in London, I offer yet one more letter which may interest the readers of your valuable paper. Brixton, though a suburb of London, is within the four-miles' radius from Charing Cross, and we are surrounded by streets; also a noisy railway runs at the end of our garden. Notwithstanding these disturbing elements, for several successive autumns we have observed the regular visits of the cuckoo. We think he comes into our garden for the numerous caterpillars which infest the wild plants which we grow, and this autumn he paid us an unusually late visit, coming in the early part of September! Last December, when the snow was thick on the ground, we saw a moorhen stalking along the garden-path. He came down to the back-door of the house. Now, we are not near any water where such a bird would be likely to live, but as we kept two geese in a pen in the garden, we think their cry may have attracted the moorhen. The following is a list of the different birds we have noticed in our narrow

13

" London   garden " : — Whitethroat,   wood-warbler, wren, thrush, titmice, rook, blackbird, starling, coletit, hedgesparrow, robin, linnet, chaffinch, and of course the misjudged sparrows in abundance.—I am, Sir, &c.,

FLORENCE E. BARLOW.

November 14, 1891.

A TAME KESTREL.

SIR,—You were kind enough two years ago to take an interest in my little tame kestrel, and I venture to hope you may now like to hear more about him. Having to leave our house in Shropshire, we took the bird by train to Staffordshire, where he apparently lost his way, as he disappeared for a fortnight. By means of advertisements in all the local papers, we found him near Crewe, where a kind platelayer had seen and secured him while stunned by flying against telegraph-wires. This year we have had occasion to move into Oxfordshire, and after a few days released " Jacky" from his cage. He seems to be afraid of again losing himself, as though he constantly takes a long and rapid flight across the park, he immediately returns to sit on a garden-bench by the side of any friend of his who may be there, or to search for an open door or window by which he may rejoin us. He cannot bear being shut out, and pecks hard at a window until he is let in. If possible, he sleeps in the house, and allows us to lift and carry him about to a more suitable perch than the head of one's bed, or the side-table in the dining-room, without opening

his eyes, or doing more than remonstrate in a subdued and sleepy voice.   Like my free but perfectly
tame rook and carrion-crow, he cannot resist talking ;
whether by day or night, all three invariably reply
when talked to or called.   " Jacky " has a low twitter-
ing note of pleasure, quite different from that of the
ordinary kestrel.   He keenly enjoys sitting on a sunny
window-seat, and letting us stroke him and smooth
his feathers.   Never does he give us the powerful
stroke of the claw with which he kills a mouse, his
only large game, in an instant.   Oddly enough, he
again, like the rook and crow, prefers boiled macaroni
to any other form of food, and will carefully remove
the raw meat or mouse on his plate in order to reach
the macaroni beneath.   Bread-and-butter he eats as
readily.   In fact, I think most birds and beasts love
a change of food.—I am, Sir, &c.,

ELLINOR C. L. CLOSE.

May 14, 1892.

AN ORNITHOLOGICAL EVICTION.

Sir,—The authorities of a small place in the Pfalz recently decided in solemn council to remove a stork's nest from the top of a very high church-steeple. The nest could only be approached outside the steeple by means of a specially fixed ladder. The storks saw the slater who had undertaken the perilous task, approaching, but waited calmly until he was quite near. Then they flew away, and the slater triumphantly removed the nest. Arrived on the ground with his trophy, he was warmly congratulated on his feat by the assembled inhabitants of the place ; but lo! at the same moment the evicted storks returned with materials for a new nest, which they began to build on the same spot without delay.—I am, Sir, &c.,

EIN THIERFREUND.

May 14, 1892.

VULTURES.

SIR,—Perhaps the following incident would interest students of natural history amongst your readers. Last week some sports took place at a station near here, one of the events being what is popularly known as a " Victoria-Cross Race "—that is, the competitors have to ride some distance, taking two or three hurdles on their way, to. a point where there are arranged a number of figures in stuffed cases, shaped like human bodies ; they then dismount, fire a round of blank cartridge, pick up a dummy each, and race back. In this case, after the sports were over the dummies were left on the ground, and in about half an hour after the ground was deserted I noticed a vulture settle on the ground close to the dummies ; in about another five minutes more than thirty had collected. The birds seemed much puzzled as they carefully inspected each lay-figure, walking from one to the next all along the line, and eventually, after sitting in a circle for a short time, flew away. These birds must have discovered the dummies by sight, though I have often heard that vultures rely on their sense of smell as well.—I am, Sir, &c.,

C. W. H. BRUCE.

September 17, 1892.

A BIRD STORY.

SIR,—I hope, although the incident may be trivial, that the little fact may interest your readers as much as it did myself when I was listening some nights ago to the little lark of whom my story tells, piping away in what the poets call "dulcet strains" of the most melodious music.

My friend James Shanock, three years ago, caught a young lark, and it has been pouring out its song ever since then from its cage, and a very sweet note it is. Some little while ago, as the afternoon was sunny, the cage was hung outside in the garden at the moment another lark was carolling in the air, and Shanock's bird rose from the cage, which was only covered with a fine net, and in which there must have been a rent, and disappeared in the direction of the other lark. My friend seeing this at once began to whistle, holding up the cage to attract his pet back again, and in a very short time down it came to his feet, and waited patiently while he gently replaced him in his cage. There were three witnesses, I believe, in this case.—I am, Sir, &c.,

G. W. HEARLE.

P.S.—The funniest thing, too, is that about the same time James Shanock's cat brought him in a little bird quite delicately, and waited for him to take it from his mouth quite uninjured. He is a great bird-lover, and it looks as if the cat, like everybody else, knew this fact.

March 11, 1893.

A BIRD STORY.

SIR,—Will you allow me to add a touching instance of courage to your pleasant bird stories? Early one morning last summer I was called to the window by a great noise among the bird people of the garden, and saw the following scene. A young blackbird was standing fascinated by a cat, who was crouched under a bush ready to spring on him. An old blackbird, on an ilex close by, was uttering loud and agitated cries, and there was a general cackle of anger and sympathy from other birds all round. After a few seconds the cat sprang on the young bird and held him down. At that instant the old bird came down on them. There was a moment's struggle, the bird beating her wings violently in the cat's face and, I think, pecking at her eyes ; then the cat jumped back to her bush, the young bird made off with long hops, and the old one flew up to the ilex, amidst a jubilant chorus of commendation which lasted quite some minutes. I never saw this before, though I have seen a robin come quite close to a cat stalking another bird, and scold and flap his wings in her face.

The ways of birds are delightful, and in a small garden you can have many by keeping earthenware saucers full of water for them to bathe in.—I am, Sir, &c.,   E. G. P.

March 25, 1893.

ANOTHER BIRD STORY.

SIR,—I have read with pleasure the stories of bird-life which appear from time to time in your paper, and as it may interest some of your readers, I send you the following narrative. Some years ago my father had a pair of common white pigeons. They were very tame, and became very much attached to him ; so much so that they were almost his constant companions, accompanying him in his walks, or when out driving. They would answer his whistle like a dog, and would alight on his proffered hand, or enter his pocket if opened for them. A sceptical friend thought they would show the same familiarity to any other person, and, to give them a fair trial, he procured a suit of clothes of the same colour as that which my father wore. Arrayed in his disguise, our sceptical friend, imitating my father's whistle as nearly as possible, whistled to the pigeons. Immediately they left their perch on the house-top and flew down to the hand held out to receive them ; but when they came within a few yards of it, they suddenly checked themselves, fluttered perplexedly for a few moments around our friend, and then flew back to the house-top. This was conclusive evidence. But a sad accident happened. One morning one of the pigeons was found upon the high-road dead, its body bearing marks of injury ; but from what cause we never knew. We carried the dead body home, and buried it in a sunny and quiet spot in the garden. For three days the surviving pigeon, with untiring energy, searched the country far and near for its mate, but in vain. It refused to touch food, and even the influence which my father usually exercised over it was gone. On the third day we found it dead in the dovecot, its little heart broken with grief by the loss of its lifelong companion. We buried it beside its mate. Since then my father has never kept pets.—I am, Sir, &c.,

WILLIAM ROSS.

April 1, 1893.

A SWISS BIRD STORY.

SIR,—Here is a bird story from Switzerland. An old peasant from the Prätigau who was dining with us to-night gave us an amusing account of a woodpecker at Couters, his home in that quiet valley. One day this bird began boring its hole in one of the logs of Herr Brosi's chalet. All night it went on working, and never stopped until at last it succeeded in getting inside the wainscoting of their "stube," or living-room. Its continual tapping began to worry Herr Brosi's wife, who said that she could not stand it. So next morning out he went and nailed a piece of wood over the hole. No sooner had he left than the woodpecker began its work again, but this time above its last hole. Again it was stopped, and so it went on until the perforated log was almost covered by Herr Brosi's pieces of board. In the end the bird's perseverance was rewarded, and it was allowed to have its own way, built its nest in the hole it had worked so hard to obtain, and since then has returned many succeeding years, and brought up numerous flourishing families. But once before its arrival, two tomtits, searching for a suitable place in which to

build, discovered this sheltered hole, which suited
their habits, and immediately began to gather materials
for lining it. When they had almost finished, the
woodpecker, discovering their intrusion, turned them
out of the domain which it had conquered with such
trouble, and again took possession.—I am, Sir, &c.,

KATHERINE SYMONDS.

July 1, 1893.

A BIRD STORY.

SIR,—I think the following may interest your readers. While staying with my father in Worcestershire this week, he told us the following story at the breakfast-table. His attention was attracted by sounds outside his dressing-room window, as of a bird in distress, and on looking out he saw a young house-martin clinging to the outside of its nest (which was built in an angle of the window), evidently very frightened, and uttering shrill cries. The parent bird, still in the nest, was firmly holding the outstretched wing of the young one with her beak ; then coming out of the nest herself, they both flew away in a downward direction, the little bird being still supported in the same way by the parent. I should be glad if any one could tell me if this is the usual way in which house-martins teach their young to fly.—I am, Sir, &c.,   B. H. BLAKE.

August 25, 1894.

HOUSE-MARTINS.

SIR,—A few days before reading the letter of your Worcestershire correspondent, in the *Spectator* of August 25th, a lady who is my neighbour here, in speaking of the flight of the young house-martins from the nests beneath her eaves, told me of the case of one lazy one (delicate, I considerately suggested), who, although fully fledged like the others of its family, refused to take the wing with them. Hearing more than the usual outcry attending the dispersal of a brood, my informant went out, and saw one of the parent birds dragging (not merely assisting) out the laggard youngster, with much clamour and gesticulation on both sides. This lady, who may be said to have passed her life with the martins beneath the mossgrown eaves, did not relate the fact as a strange one, but assured me that such an instance was common enough in her experience, and that she had always regarded it as an example of parental discipline on the part of the swallows. The questionable sympathy of the animal world with its infirmer members is sufficiently known, so that (as in the case above) the grip of your correspondent's elder bird upon the wing of the younger may not impossibly have been a prolonged, because much-needed enforcement of the lesson intended. Of course, as is suggested, it may just as probably have been a manifestation of helpful sympathy, as instances of this too are frequent ; but in either case the illustration of parental virtue would be an equally strong one. The piece of behaviour referred to, however, hardly seems sufficiently common to warrant the supposition that instruction in the use of wings is any more *generally* necessary in the world of youthful house-martins than in others with which we are more directly familiar.—I am, Sir, &c.,

ALGERNON GISSING.

September 8, 1894.

A BIRD STORY.

SIR,—This episode in the life of an Australian bird, received in a letter from Queensland, may be interesting to your readers :—" Since you take an interest in my birds, you may like to know that the jackass has come back, after an absence of nearly three weeks. One wet evening just before sundown, I heard their voices ʿquite near, and saw two birds on a stump. Looking through the glasses I saw that one of them had a cut wing. I went out, and there was my wandering boy, opening his mouth for his supper, and quite ready to go home with me. The wild birds, however, do not like the arrangement, and one of them has spent almost all her time since (about three days) in trying to get him away again. She is there early and late in the trees near the house and on the posts of the fence, calling and persuading, and he answers her, evidently arguing the matter. When we are all inside, she even comes on to the verandah, and brings him a choice variety of worms and centipedes. This morning she brought him a lizard, quite eight inches long. I feel that great consideration is due to her. She must have saved his life, for he had not the least idea of foraging for himself when he went away. The others are well. ' Choy,' the butcher-bird, nearly did for himself a few days ago by hobbling himself with a skein of red sewing silk. He got it twisted round both his feet, and then round and round the back of his tongue, which became quite swollen and black. Dr. D—— was hastily called. I held his mouth open, and with the help of scissors and crochet-needle he was set free much subdued."—I am, Sir, &c.,

L. G.

June 22, 1895.

INSECTS AND REPTILES.

THE INTELLIGENCE OF BEES.

SIR,—I have just read your extremely interesting paper on the power of bees to communicate with each other. I do not know if the following story—the truth of which I vouch for—is of any value as an illustration.

Some years ago a boy playing with a jackdaw in a large garden where bees were kept came near the hives, and the bird hopped on to the little platform in front of one of these houses. It was about sunset, and the bees had nearly all returned from their day's outing among the heather ; the few late arrivals, as soon as they alighted at their own door, were rapidly despatched by Jack's sharp beak. This lasted for a minute or two, when some bees were observed issuing from the door of the hive, and the bird assailed them at once, and killed them as fast as they crawled out. Then there was a pause, no bee going out or coming in, as far as the boy could see, but he heard a humming

sound inside the hive, and immediately there came
out of the low doorway a strong band of bees, so close
to each other, that poor Jack, work as hard as he
could, had no chance with them.   He was attacked
in the rear, and took to flight ; but rapidly as he flew,
the bees were faster, and a cloud spread out like a
sheet, pursued him for nearly a mile, when they over-
took him in the air, and the boy saw his favourite pet
fall fluttering to the ground, where he picked him up,
his eyes closed, and his head swollen to twice its
natural size.

In this case the bees knew how to communicate
" intelligence," and how to act.—I am, Sir, &c.,

DAVID DOUGLAS.

June 19, 1875.

THE INTERPRETATION OF ANIMAL CHARACTER.

SIR,—In your very interesting article on "The Interpretation of Animal Character" you thus sum up your remarks on Sir John Lubbock's observations of the habits of the particular carpenter-wasp described by him:—"If there be no power of adaptation of resources to meet new difficulties, it is incredible that there can be arithmetical capacity enough for counting ten. We should take the power of an animal to meet unexpected emergencies of a simple kind as the most elementary of all tests of reason as distinguished from mere instinct. The ant or the beaver which makes good the injuries of whatever kind which happens to its settlement, certainly reasons." As bearing on the question raised, may I be permitted to recall the very singular case recorded by Huber of the conduct of bees whose hives had been plundered by the moth *Acherontia atropos* (the well-known death's-head moth)? This moth, as most of your entomological readers may be aware, is singular among *Lepidoptera* in its capacity of uttering a peculiar piping sound, closely resembling a sound emitted by the queen-bee in certain circumstances, which has a most extraordinary effect on the inmates of the hives. Huber thus describes it :—" The effects are very remarkable. As soon as the sound was heard, bees that had been employed in plucking, biting, and chasing the queen about, hung down their heads, and remained altogether motionless ; and whenever she had recourse to this attitude and sound, they operated upon them in the same manner." One summer, the beekeepers in the district of Switzerland where Huber resided, were much puzzled to account for the apparent bad success of their bees. The season had been good, the bees were healthy and active, but the hives, when lifted, were very light. The results of all their industry were most disappointing. A watch was set upon the hives, when the cause was soon discovered. In the twilight of the evening, the moth I have mentioned, which was unusually plentiful that year, was detected in large numbers entering the hives. This they were able to do with impunity by their producing the singular noise which I have described. Apparently the same effects were produced upon the bees as were caused by the similar noise emitted by the queen. In this way it appeared the moths had been successful in their plundering the hives. When this was discovered, the proprietors of the hives placed before the entrance a grating of wire with apertures sufficient to admit the bees, but too small to allow of the entrance of the moth. The consequence was an immediate improvement in the yield of honey. But what seemed very singular, those hives which were not so protected also shared in the improvement. On examination, a most singular discovery was made. Behind the entrance of the unprotected hive—unprotected by the owner—it was found that the bees had constructed a double wall of a mixture of wax and propolis, the one close behind the other, each of them perforated with apertures through which the bees found admission to the hives, but those of the inner wall placed not opposite to the apertures of the outer wall, so that the bee had to turn in the narrow space between the two walls, an operation impossible to the moth, even had it been able to push itself through the hole in the outer wall. In this way the bees had successfully defended themselves, as their neighbours had been defended by their proprietors. This would seem most completely to answer your test,—"The power of an animal to meet an emergency of a simple kind." Surely, one would say, here is as ample proof of reason as is given by the ant or by the beaver in making good an injury to its settlement. The bees proved that they knew the cause of their unsuccessful labour. They reasoned—shall we say?—what would keep out the depredator ; but their knowledge and their reason were not strong enough to overcome the singular instinct which caused them to lie still and motionless under the influence of the plunderer's music, instead of stinging her to death in a moment, as they would have done to any other intruder.—I am, Sir, &c., D. McL.

[This fact, if well authenticated, is not only very

remarkable in itself, but would also prove that bees are not deaf to the higher notes, though Sir John Lubbock believes them to be deaf to the notes which man hears most easily.—ED. *Spectator.*]

February 26, 1887.

A WASP POLICEMAN.

SIR,—The letter from Eastbourne of March 26th reminds me of an incident which interested us very much last summer. My house is close to a large wood, so that we are troubled by swarms of flies. I had cut off a bough from an oak in the garden, and some time after remarked that the cut surface was wet with sap, which some half-dozen wasps were greedily devouring. The nearer boughs were covered with flies ; they made persistent attempts to obtain a share of the sap, but in vain, for they were constantly driven away by one of the wasps, which made no attempt itself to eat, but attended ·steadily to its policeman's duty. Every now and then all the wasps rushed to and fro, and we fancied that at these times the policeman was relieved. Though we could not be sure about this, there was no room for doubt as to the reality of the police duty, for none of the other wasps tried to drive the flies away.—I am, Sir, &c.,

R. S. CULLEY.

April 5, 1890.

A HERMIT WASP.

SIR,—All through the past winter a solitary wasp has been noticed in the garden here. On every occasion when the sun made his appearance, the wasp was also in evidence.

A few days ago, on turning over a board which has been constantly used for the passage of a wheelbarrow across a ditch, I discovered the hermit's cell. The nest is of the usual grey, paper-like material, and perfectly formed, but is only about the size of a small walnut. Having evicted the tenant, I appropriated his domicile, and a more beautiful and perfect specimen of insect architecture I have never seen.

Can you or any of your readers inform me if the circumstance is unusual?—I am, Sir, &c.,

CHARLES M. CLARKE, LL.D.

May 24, 1890.

THE LIZARD'S LOVE OF MUSIC.

SIR,—With reference to your interesting article on
" Animal Æsthetics," I should like to give you one of
my own experiences. When in Switzerland two years
ago I made the acquaintance of some lizards, living
in the crevices of one of the sunny walls of our garden.
As I had somewhere heard that lizards have a good
ear for music, I resolved to prove the fact ; so one
afternoon, armed with a small musical-box, I wended
my steps to their tomato-covered home. Before I
had finished the first tune, a considerable audience
had collected—an audience it was a pleasure to play
to, for the lizards were far more attentive than most
human beings. Out peered head after head, a little
on one side, in a listening attitude. I gave my little
friends a musical entertainment (varied by whistling)
nearly every day, and before long they got much
bolder, and would venture right out of their holes, and ·
lie motionless on the broad ledge of the wall, their
bright black eyes half-closed as a rule, but opening
now and then to give me a lazy wink of enjoyment.—
I am, Sir, &c.,   L. I. A.

June 20, 1891.

INSECTS AND MUSIC.

SIR,—In your article, "Orpheus at the Zoo," in the *Spectator* of October 3rd, the tarantula's non-appreciation of music is contrasted with the scorpion's very sensitive ear for the violin. I have studied the habits of the scorpion for many years, and have often noticed how very sensitive scorpions are to the most delicate sound, musical or otherwise. Under the thorax the scorpion has two comb-like appendages, which are the antennæ (pectinatæ). It is pretty well settled by physiologists and entomologists that in insects the antennæ represent the organs of hearing. These delicate structures are easily affected by the vibrations of sound, and there can be no doubt whatever that they are also affected by sounds quite inaudible to the human ear. The slightest vibration of the atmosphere, from any cause whatever, at once puts in motion the delicate structures which compose the antennæ, to which organs insects owe the power of protecting themselves against danger, as well as the means of recognising the approach of one another. Spiders have wonderful eyesight, but I am quite sure that the scorpion's vision, notwithstanding his six eyes, is far from being acute. It is very difficult to catch a spider with a pair of forceps, but a scorpion can be easily captured, if no noise is made. Spiders see their prey before they are caught in the web ; but the scorpion makes no movement whatever to seize flies or cockroaches until they indicate their where-abouts by movements. This being the case, it can readily be understood how easily the scorpion may be roused into motion by the vibrations of music, as described in the article alluded to. If a tuning-fork be sounded on the table on which I keep my caged scorpion, he at once becomes agitated, and strikes out viciously with his sting. On touching him with the vibrating tuning-fork, he stings it, and then coils him-self up, as scorpions do when hedged in. In Jamaica, the negroes believe that scorpions know their name ; so they never call out, " See a scorpion," when they meet with one on the ground or wall, for fear of his escaping. They thus indirectly recognise the scorpion's delicate appreciation of sound ; but if you wish to stop a scorpion in his flight, blow air on him from the mouth, and he at once coils himself up. I have repeatedly done this ; but with the spider it has a contrary effect. Music charms a snake into silence, as the experiments at the Zoo and elsewhere prove ; but the agitated contortions and writhings of the scorpions when roused by the sound of the violin only prove that they are roused by the vibrations of sound caused by music, and this would happen if they were disturbed by the discordant sounds of a penny-trumpet, or any other unmusical instrument.—I am, Sir, &c., JASPER CARGILL, M.D.

December 19, 1891.

HAVE SNAKES THE POWER OF SCENT?

SIR,—In the *Spectator* of March 18th you head a snake incident by asking, " Have Snakes the Power of Scent?"   That some attractive sympathy exists amongst them seems evident. Some years ago a large English snake was killed and left on the garden-path near to the house.   Having a great dread of the reptiles, and the curious desire to look upon the "horror," I went to see the dead serpent.   It lay lifeless upon the stony path ; but moving about its wounded head was a living snake, apparently of the same species, and too much engrossed with the grim object to notice my presence.   Some sympathy must have attracted the shy creature to its mate.—I am, Sir, &c.,

C. S. LUNN.

April 1, 1893.

FROGS AND WASPS.

SIR,—As you and your readers seem interested in odds-and-ends of natural history, I send you one which may be worth publishing. Some time ago I discovered accidentally that frogs are voracious eaters of wasps. I have in my garden a tank for watering, with an island of rock-work, which is a favourite haunt of frogs. The wasps just now are carrying on a raid against my fruit, and when I wish to gratify at once my revenge and my frogs, I catch a marauder between a postcard and an inverted wine-glass, carry him off to the tank, wet his wings to prevent his flying, and set him on the rock-work before the frogs. After a moment's pause, a frog advances, and in an instant the wasp has disappeared, drawn into the frog's mouth by a single dart of his long tongue. Occasionally the wasp reappears wholly or partially, having made it unpleasant for the frog ; but he is almost always swallowed in the end. Usually, convulsive movements may be noticed in the frog's throat and body, as though the process of deglutition were not quite easy ; but that they like the diet is evident from the fact that a single smallish frog has been known to take three wasps one after another. Indeed, it is remarkable what very small frogs, quite infants, will swallow a wasp with avidity.   This afternoon a tiny frog swallowed a full-grown wasp, when a big relative went for him quite savagely, like a big schoolboy thrashing a small one for presuming to be helped before him.—I am, Sir, &c.,

R. E. BARTLETT.

September 2, 1893.

ANIMAL ETIQUETTE.

SIR,—Your article on "Animal Etiquette," in the *Spectator* of March 2nd, does not notice a habit prevailing in the bee world which seems to deserve that name. It is that bees in a hive never turn their backs on the queen. The members of her retinue (the "ladies in waiting") are ranged dutifully round her, and the same order is maintained as the queen passes on her way. One of the surest ways of finding the queen (no easy task) is to look for a cluster of bees the various members of which are standing in a circle, their bodies radiating outwards like the spokes of a wheel. It is believed that queens do not use their stings, except in a battle royal—a conflict with a rival They may be handled at all times with impunity, even put in the mouth (*experto crede*) without showing any resentment, save by a bite! In a royal sister alone they seem to recognise a "foeman worthy of their steel." Is this etiquette too? or has it stretched to the verge of prejudice?

It is true bees have been known to kill a new queen by suffocation, technically called "encasing," but the process has been explained as denoting an exuberance of loyalty and joy at finding a new sovereign, who is thus literally "smothered by kindness"—Qy., kisses. —I am, Sir, &c., L. T. RENDELL.

March 9, 1895.

VARIETY OF CHARACTER IN INSECTS.

SIR,—I have just read the latest "dog-story" in a letter addressed to you in the *Spectator* of January 12th. The following sentence in this letter—"To prove that the disposition of animals are as varied as those of human beings," recalls to my mind a fact about insects which I think would interest some people. No one who has ever kept animals as pets can doubt their varied temperaments, but some insects also manifest a like difference. When I was a child I often amused myself with teasing spiders ; I never hurt them. I would throw a small piece of leaf into a nice newly-made web and watch the result. Some spiders would rush out in a terrible rage and, quite regardless of the beautiful new web, run right across it and thrust out the offending object, doing much damage to the new fly-trap in its course; others of less hasty temper and of a more reflective turn of mind would come quietly a short distance, look at the object for a minute, and then quietly retire. Then sometimes a spider would be in the centre of his web, and when he saw me looking at him he would rush away and hide himself, or he would tremble so as to violently shake his web. These facts are perfectly true, and many were the spiders whom I used to visit. These last I should call highly nervous insects.—I am, Sir, &c., C. J.

January 19, 1895.

SAGACITY OF A QUEEN-BEE.

SIR,—As you sometimes insert incidents illustrative of natural history, the following may be interesting to some of your readers :—About three weeks ago I had a small cast of bees. Not knowing the hive from which they had come, and wishing them to find their own way back, I proceeded to adopt the usual method of capturing the queen. After throwing the bees on to the sheet three times, I succeeded in finding her and securing her between a wine-glass and a flat plate of glass. I liberated one by one the few workers I had inclosed with her. I then took her to my study, intending to destroy her with chloroform. However, in slipping the saturated tuft of cotton-wool under the glass, she was too sharp for me, darted out, and, making straight for the open window, escaped. My study is in the front of the vicarage, and the swarm were in the kitchen-garden at the back. I at once ran to them to see if she had returned straight, but found them in the state of wild confusion which indicates absence of a queen. After watching them for some time, I left them. Returning in about an hour, I found them still rushing about. I went to look at something else in the garden, and returned in about five minutes to find the aspect of affairs quite altered. The confusion had ceased, and they presented every appearance of a newly-hived swarm, some forming a small cluster in the place where they had originally swarmed (a beanstalk), and others moving calmly in and out of the hive. Next morning I found the hive empty and the cluster fully formed. Once more I hived them, and they are now going on steadily with every appearance of having a queen among them, though I have not thought well again to disturb them in search of her. Had she on escaping risen straight up so as to surmount the roof and beech-hedge interposed between her and the back garden, she would have been about eighty yards from the swarm. She took about an hour and a half to find them. But she did·find them at last. I shall not lengthen my already too long communication by mentioning the several interesting conclusions to which the facts point.—I am, Sir, &c., USHER B. MILES.

August 3, 1895.

VARIETY OF CHARACTER IN INSECTS.

SIR,—For the chance of your caring to insert in the *Spectator* my comment on a letter signed " C. J.," in the *Spectator* of January 19th, I beg to say, as a jealous observer of Nature from my boyhood, that spiders and their marvellous ingenuity attracted my attention in very early days. When a boy I watched the process of the geometric species in forming their webs, and waited till they had constructed them before I ventured to feed their exhausted frames with a fly. It is not in the power of man to do justice to these insects, though we can learn something from their precision. Words are powerless to describe it, and certainly no human power can properly understand it. Kirby and Spence, in their work on Entomology, did a good deal to help one to entertain some faint idea of what is in store for those who try to appreciate insect creation—to my regret I hear this work is out of print. But referring to " C. J.'s " letter above alluded to, I suggest that the tremor he attributes to his spider, was due to a very different cause than his august presence. It would be a pleasure to me to go into details—to narrate the particulars of the formation of the web, which is mathematically planned, and every tissue of it proceeds from the "anus" (I presume I may call it) of the spider's body. Therefore any substance (if it be but a midge) lighting on that tissue, by telegraphic communication as it were, affects the person of the spider ; though, maybe, inclosed " in his little parlour " far away. It is that which brings him out of his seclusion ! and down he comes, not on his victim (for I doubt whether his eyesight is of much avail), but he can feel, and goes straight to the centre of his web, fixes his eight claws each on the radii of the web, gives each a good honest tug, and the victim responds with a shrug, and straight Mr. Spider waits upon him. This, I believe, is the tremor your friend refers to.—I am, Sir, &c.,   GEORGE MILLER.

January 24th.

WEB-SHAKING BY SPIDERS.

SIR,—May I suggest a doubt as to the interpretation given by Mr. Veasey, as well as that given by your correspondent of January 19th, of the curious web-shaking of spiders? I have often provoked and watched this shaking, and, as far as my experience goes, I have never yet seen it as a response to the action of real wind. The shaking seems to me only performed when the spider fears or suspects an enemy, and the aim of the spider I have always taken to be to make itself less definitely visible to this supposed enemy. The motion is so rapid that only a blurred patch represents the spider's body to one's eye; and I believe the action to be entirely protective in origin, with perhaps a dash of temper superadded.—I am, Sir, &c.,   E. H.

OTHER BEASTS.

HORSES, COWS, AND DONKEYS.

A CLEVER DONKEY.

SIR,—As I am sure your sympathies are not confined to dogs, though at present they only have appeared in your paper, I am going to ask you for a small space for just one anecdote of *my* favourite animal —the donkey, an animal so universally snubbed and looked down upon, that it seems almost a duty to make public anything that tends to show he is by no means so stupid as he is generally thought to be.

Biped friends of mine are at the seaside, and the donkey I am anxious to see in print, because of the credit he reflects on his race generally (intellectually, if not morally), was engaged for an hour to take two children up and down the parade, but when it came to the turn of the second to mount, " Neddy " fell so suddenly and distressingly lame, that the little girl refused to have her ride, but the boy in charge of the

donkey assured those in charge of the children that
it was only a "trick" he had ; that he "disliked
going up and down the parade," and always "fell
lame" when required to do it ; and the truth of the
statement was tested by holding a crust to Neddy's
nose and running off with it in an opposite direction,
when Neddy cantered briskly after it, his lameness as
suddenly and easily put off as it had been put on.
Now, for a donkey, this was rather clever, if not quite
so interesting as the story of the dog that tried to
fill the void in its heart—and its kennel—by adopting
a young pigeon, or so clever as the dogs told of lately
in the *Spectator*, that went to the confectioner's with
the money in their mouths for their dinner, insisting,
too, upon having their money's worth—a good dinner
when they had a whole penny, but expecting only
half the quantity when they were "hard-up," and only
took a halfpenny. And I was once so very subject
to sudden headaches and "pain in the side" whenever it was time to go to school, that I naturally
sympathise with Neddy's sudden lameness when
required to go up and down a parade ; and so many,
I fancy, must be able to sympathise with him for the
same reason, that surely he is deserving of a place
where perhaps no donkey—on four legs—has ever
appeared before.—I am, Sir, &c.,   W.

May 19, 1877.

A CLEVER HORSE.

SIR,—The method adopted by "Topsy" in opening the door is not only simple, as mentioned by your correspondent, but, I think, not uncommon. I have seen dogs do the same thing, and once had a horse who, on the top door of his loose-box being opened, would not only undo with his mouth the latch of the bottom part of the door, but would even draw the bolt beneath it in order to get out. This horse lived to be twenty-three years old. I have also seen a cat turn the handle of the kitchen-door in order to gain an entrance; this he did by holding it between his front paws, the handle of course being, like others frequently used, extremely loose.—I am, Sir, &c.,

A. H. D.

June 6, 1885.

A SOCIABLE HORSE.

SIR,—The following story of equine 'cuteness may interest your readers:—A friend of mine, having more horses than his normal amount of stabling would accommodate, put up two of them in an old hovel, temporarily divided into two compartments by three bars of wood stretching from side to side. One of these beasts, an iron-grey cob, was found every morning in the same compartment as his fellow, and for a long time the manner in which he got from his own to his neighbour's stall remained a mystery. One morning, however, he was found by the coach-man, who happened to look into the hovel rather earlier than usual, lying on his side under the lowest of the three bars, with half his body on one side and half on the other, vigorously " scratting himself through," as the coachman expressed it. A few shouts hastened his movements, and he quickly worked himself clean through, and began calmly munching by the side of his companion.—I am, Sir, &c., F. S. ARNOLD.

July 30, 1887.

A CLEVER COW.

SIR,—The following, received from a correspondent writing from Dieppe, is interesting in its way, and bears upon the subject of your recent article, "Animal Character."

"F. A. T." writes, under date October, 1888 :—

"I saw a very curious thing the other day. We were walking in the country past a lot of large orchards, and we noticed that the cows that were feeding in them had their heads fastened down by a kind of bearing-rein, so that they could graze but could not raise their heads to eat the trees. While we were looking, we noticed a cow go up to an apple-tree and wedge-in the stem between her horns and neck, and deliberately shake the tree and bring down a shower of apples ; she and the others ate them up, and then she went to another tree and shook that, and so on. It was the funniest thing I ever saw : she always chose young trees that would shake easily. I pointed it out to a Frenchwoman standing near, and she said she had often watched them, and thought how clever the cow was. It was always the same cow that did it, and she did it as systematically as a schoolboy, never attempting to shake an old, stiff tree."

There seems to be more reason in French cows than in ours. A scientific gentleman wrote to a paper the other day to say that blackbirds did not eat fruit because they liked it, but because they were thirsty, and recommended we should place pans of water on the gravel walks and so save our garden fruit. A cottager in Montgomeryshire being told of this interesting fact, replied in the dialect of that part of the country—"Dern the bruts; they cross the bruck to come to my geërding." It would thus appear that the character of animals varies with the country, and that of blackbirds with the county.—I am, Sir, &c.,

T. W. T.

October 13, 1888.

WILD HORSES' COMMUNICATIONS WITH EACH OTHER.

SIR,—I have read with interest your articles on the instinct of cattle. That cattle and horses can communicate intelligence to each other, and are endowed with a certain amount of reasoning faculty, the following facts are pretty conclusive proof. I once purchased a station on which a large number of cattle and horses had gone wild. To get the cattle in, I fenced the permanent water (a distance of twenty miles), leaving traps at intervals. At first this answered all right, but soon the cattle became exceedingly cautious about entering the traps, waiting outside for two or three nights before going in, and if they could smell a man or his tracks, not going in at all. At last they adopted a plan which beat me. A mob would come to the trap-gate, and one would go in and drink, and come out ; and then another would do the same, and so on, till all had watered. They had evidently arrived at the conclusion that I would not catch *one* and frighten all the others away.

To get in the wild horses, six hundred of which

were running on a large plain (about twenty thousand acres), I erected a stockyard, with a gradually widening lane, in a hollow where it could not easily be seen, and by stationing horsemen at intervals on the plain, galloped the wild horses in. My first hunt (which lasted for some days) was successful, the wild horses heading towards the mouth of the lane without much difficulty ; but, of course, some escaped by charging back at the stockyard gate, and in other ways. My second hunt, about a month later, was a failure ; every mob of horses on the plain seemed to know where the yard was, and would not head that way. This seems to show that the horses that escaped from the first hunt told all the others where the stockyard was.—I am, Sir, &c.,   ANDREW J. OGILVIE.

December 19, 1891.

A CLEVER PONY.

SIR,—*À propos* of your interesting article on the
"Animal Sense of Humour," in the *Spectator* of
October 1st, allow me to send you a case of grim
humour displayed a short time since by a pony
belonging to a friend.   It had been pouring hard
all day, everything was soaking, and the poor pony
looked in vain for a dry spot to lie on.   After
evidently deliberate thought, it went up to a cow
who had been lying in one place for a long while,
and gave her a most vicious kick ; this he repeated
several times, until at last she was compelled regret-
fully to rise, whereupon the pony promptly lay down
in the very spot occupied and kept dry by the cow.
—I am, Sir, &c.,   B. F. J.

October 8, 1892.

SAGACITY OF THE HORSE.

SIR,—An instance of the extraordinary sagacity and fidelity of a horse may interest the readers of the *Spectator.* The account appeared in the *Pioneer of India* two or three months ago, and was reproduced in the *Royal Engineers' Journal* on June 1st. I quote from the latter paper :—" With reference to the murderous attack made upon Lieutenant Robertson, R.E., by a youthful Ghazi at Gulistan, it appears that the former was out riding and was joined by the Ghazi, who was also on horseback. Both entered into friendly conversation, and shortly afterwards put their horses to a trial of speed, in which Lieutenant Robertson outstripped his rival, when the Ghazi being a short distance behind, suddenly drew his tulwar and inflicted a severe gash on Lieutenant Robertson's neck, and otherwise wounding his hand, which he had raised to ward off the Ghazi's attack. . . . It is stated that when Lieutenant Robertson fell off his horse, and was lying on the ground, bleeding profusely, the faithful animal protected his master from further injury by kicking at the Ghazi and attempting to bite him. But for this remarkable behaviour on the part of Lieutenant Robertson's horse, it is supposed that the Ghazi would have probably hacked Lieutenant Robertson to death."

I hear from a private correspondent that this account is quite accurate, and also that two Indian boys, hidden among trees close by, saw the attack made on Mr. Robertson, and managed to stop a passing train. The Ghazi at once rode off, but was caught soon afterwards, identified, and sentenced to be hanged. The wounded officer was put into the train, and taken to the hospital at Quetta, where he was recovering from the severe injuries he had received.—I am, Sir, &c.,   A. E. H.

July 9, 1892.

A SAGACIOUS HORSE.

SIR,—While at Champéry, in Switzerland, this last summer, I saw a curious incident. A shepherd was with his flock of sheep some way up the mountainside. Instead of a sheep-dog he had a horse which acted in that capacity. The shepherd spoke to the horse, who at once galloped off and brought in the stray sheep. He then returned to his master for further orders, which he carried out in most exemplary fashion.—I am, Sir, &c.,

R. H. BOMPAS.

February 9, 1895.

ANIMAL VISION.

SIR,—I am tempted by the letter which appears in the *Spectator* of June 29th to think that others besides myself are interested in the subject of " Animal Colour-Vision," and therefore, though rather late, to send you the following particulars :— About twenty-six years ago my father, who, though already over seventy, still hunted a good deal in Northamptonshire, took up there a little horse bred by himself, who was a great pet of mine, and much coveted by me as a hack. After one or two seasons he returned to me, but I do not think I should have got him had he not proved more excitable with hounds than, at that time, suited my father. My father has frequently told me that if he came down in the morning in a *dark* coat, he could at least get to the meet in peace, but if he wore a *red* one, " Cuckoo" was always in a dance from the moment they started. My father was used to horses all his life, and a pretty good judge of what they could or could not understand. I think he looked on this instance of "knowingness" as worth telling, but not as anything very wonderful. I live a good deal with my dogs, but regret to say I have no like tales to tell of them. What does strike me very much is the very varying degrees in which individuals, even of the same breed, are guided by scent or sight respectively; some, though they can see quite well, seem to me hardly to *look* at all, while others evidently notice things at a considerable distance, and even high up in the air.—I am, Sir, &c.,

HANGHER DOWN.

July 6, 1895.

STORY OF A DONKEY.

SIR,—As your readers seem interested in stories of affection and fidelity in animals, I think it possible you might consider the enclosed worthy of insertion in your paper. The truth of the story is guaranteed by several persons whose names are given, but not for publication.

A donkey cast off by a costermonger as useless, and in a miserable condition, was found by a young gentleman, who brought it into his garden. Being kindly treated, it by and by recovered itself and became a great favourite. But the presence of so large an animal in a garden became naturally very inconvenient, and an aunt of the gentleman in question, residing at Blackheath, offered the creature an asylum in her field, and there it remained peaceful and happy. By and by the compassionate lady introduced a pony into the field, in much the same condition as the donkey had once been. The two became much attached to each other, and passed their days in a state of blissful quietness probably unknown before in their suffering and hard-working lives. Not many weeks ago the donkey died, and standing over him, in mute but eloquent grief, the pony was seen licking the insensible remains of his poor friend. He could not be induced to leave the place, or take any food, and even after the body of his beloved companion had been committed to the earth, he was seen standing by and constantly pawing the ground, as though entreating him to rise and bear him company as of old.—I am, Sir, &c., E. E.

October 19, 1895.

MONKEYS.

THE MARMOSET MONKEY.

SIR,—While I write a small marmoset monkey—
length about six inches—disports himself freely in
a sumach tree near to a sunny wall in our garden,
amusing himself with catching newly fledged moths,
small spiders, or any other specimens of the insect
tribe that may come in his way. This season these
are curiously few and far between, and he will, *faute
de mieux,* even eat earwigs, or, as Lord Tennyson's
North-country " Spinster " calls them, " battle-twigs."
Query, which is the more correct term of the two, or
the least incorrect?

Seeing that Marmie finds nothing more of an edible
kind, I offer him a fresh-gathered pea-pod, and
he eagerly gnaws the end, inserts a tiny hand, and
helps himself to one pea after another, devouring it
with avidity, all but the skin, which he wisely rejects
as tough and indigestible. These little monkeys are
very nice in their food—as particular as any epicure
in their choice of kind and condition. Everything
they take must be of the freshest and best. Only the

ripest and sweetest fruit, only the cream off the milk, only the purest water, only live insects, will suit Marmie. His infinite delight in being in the open air is quite beyond description. He will climb up or downstairs to get at me, in the hope of inducing me to take him into the garden. If shut up in his cage, he will cry like a child, with the same object in view; and to drive out in a carriage is as great a pleasure to him as to any child. He will look from the window all the time, and the little head works this way and that, the bright eyes taking in all the surroundings. Anything that attracts his special notice—a red parasol, a white horse, a bright-coloured van, a child with a skipping-rope—is greeted with a vivacious "Chip, chip!" and an upward look for sympathy at each passing excitement.

There is, perhaps, no other garden in England around the paths of which a little marmoset has daily gambolled during the late warm summer weather, finding its meals *al fresco*, in the shape of small snails and slugs, spiders, caterpillars, and beetles. He is very fond of the woodlouse, too ("cheeselog," an old servant calls them), which is fortunate, since it may be found in the absence of all else.

One is usually taught to suppose that these little delicate pets must be fed on bread-and-milk (which they appear to hate, or at least only take when driven to it by sheer hunger), and kept in close confinement in a warm room, or a greenhouse at most. But certainly where it is possible to let them enjoy the fresh open air in warm weather, with a natural diet of insects, it apparently suits them, and gives them a sense of enjoyment of life which is the nearest approach to their happy existence in their native, wild, beautiful woods of Brazil that we can give them.—I am, Sir, &c.,   BEATRICE BATTY.

July 17, 1886.

THE MARMOSET.

SIR,—May I again, through the medium of your widely-read paper, say a few words in favour of the thousands of little helpless marmosets which are annually taken from their tropical native land to die in colder climates?

Having kept these beautiful little creatures through several winters, and closely observed them, I have come to the conclusion that one reason of the mortality amongst them in their foreign surroundings is that in the anxiety to keep them sufficiently warm, they are kept too much without the fresh air to which they have been used, and which they evidently delight in and pine for. The one I now have had for two winters is in perfect health and condition. This very day he frisked round the garden in spite of frost on the ground, chirruping in the sunshine. Throughout this severe winter he has been out of doors on each sunny day for a short time. Within doors the temperature has been kept at about 60° or 62° for him as far as possible, night and day. A gas-burner left alight at night in a previously warmed room is sufficient for this, and " Marmie " sleeps in a box-cage,.

furnished with plenty of cotton-wool and light flannel wraps, as well as a small flannel-covered wool-mattress, with which he entirely blocks the entrance to his nest after he gets in for the night, thus effectually excluding all draughts. He accepts as his bedfellow, with decided approbation, and generally kissing it and whistling to it, a furry monkey-doll, which is his constant plaything during the day, and which doubtless helps to keep him warm. The other difficulty—of diet—has been got over by supplying him with common garden-snails—which he requires to have neatly and carefully cracked for him—since other insect food has been unattainable. He eats two or three of these during the day, or, at least, portions of them. It is the white muscle that he chiefly cares for, the other parts being apparently less digestible. With the addition of gum-arabic, prickly-pears, bananas, angelica, and the juice of stewed apples, together with fresh pure water and a little cream, he has "eked out an existence." The quantity taken of any food is infinitesimally small; but he is well and strong and active, intensely pretty and amusing, and apparently happy and content; although, could he speak so as to be generally understood, he would certainly explain that he prefers the season when spiders and flies, beetles and grubs, and young green peas and beans, are to be had in plenty, and when the temperature within and without is that of a genial summer heat.—I am, Sir, &c.,

BEATRICE BATTY.

February 26, 1887.

THE LANGUAGE OF THE MARMOSET.

Sir,—Some attention has been aroused by the recent attempt to reproduce monkey-talk by means of the phonograph. It is perhaps not generally known that in a little book, published nearly a hundred years ago, at the sign (strangely enough) of the Tour de Babel, on the Quai Voltaire, Paris, a French writer made an endeavour to reduce the chatter of the tiny marmoset to articulate translatable language. The whistle, or *ouistiti*, from which this little creature has its French name, he describes truly as a long, sharp, piercing sound, repeated two or three times, signifying the want of something or some one. I would add to this, that it is evidently the call used by one to the other. A very young one that I had always cried "Ouistititi, ouistititi," to the older one for help, if it thought itself in danger. "Ghriii," a long-drawn high tone, he translates into "come." All those that I have possessed have thus called me to come to them. "Guenakiki" expresses, he says, terrible fear; "Trouakki," violent, despairing grief; "Trouagno," intense pain, "save me." One that had broken its leg thus warned me of it. "Krrrreoeoeo," often repeated, means very happy indeed ; "Keh," a little better ; "Korrie," annoyed, disturbed ; "Ococo," deep terror ; "Anic," feebly and melodiously uttered, means help! protect! "Quih," "I want something very much"; "Quouééé," despair of escaping some danger—this sound I have often heard all my marmosets make at the sight of anything strange to them, or which reminded them of some known danger.

The above, and other expressions, fanciful as they may appear to some, yet have a clear meaning to those who, like Pierquin de Gembloux, are accustomed to watch and observe "dumb" animals closely, and who, as the present writer feels, can thus arrive at understanding even their mute appeals for help, sympathy, companionship, or kindness.—I am, Sir, &c.,

BEATRICE BATTY.

April 23, 1892.

THE MARMOSET.

SIR,—Those who have followed with any degree of
interest my suggestions and experiences in the matter
of feeding the marmoset, so often dying of decline in
this country from the lack of suitable nourishment
rather than from cold, may be glad to know that they
will relish oysters—at least so I find to be the case
with the one which I have had for some seven and a
half years, and which continues in good health, in
spite of the severity of the season. The frost renders
the procuring of snails difficult; and the obtaining of
any variety in the way of insect diet is in winter
almost impossible. My pet, "Marmie," will eat the
left half of an oyster at luncheon-time with evident
enjoyment; and with his tongue and tiny teeth will
tear morsels from a pheasant bone after the manner
of a cat. Live shrimps are not to be had from the
fishmongers. They will not bear transportation.
But where they can be had on the coast, the marmoset need not want a change of food. "Marmie"
likes nothing better, when he can get them. During
the cold weather a gas-burner is left alight in the
room in which he sleeps; and although the tempera-

17

ture has been as low as 50°, he does not seem to suffer, probably because he is carefully fed and well wrapped up.   He prefers his sugar-water with the chill off, and he has a warm bed of flannel and cotton-wool, with an extra blanket, all aired at the fire night and morning, and a green-baize cover to his cage.

Hoping that my letter, if you are so good as to publish it, may help to give some little marmosets a happy New Year, and wishing you the same.—I am, Sir, &c.,   BEATRICE BATTY.

January 14, 1893.

ELEPHANTS.

A TRICKY ELEPHANT.

SIR,—As an instance of the sagacity of the elephant, the following anecdote may be of interest. It was told me by Mr. Quay,—at the time a non-commissioned officer in the 1st Battalion of the 60th Rifles, but now one of her Majesty's Yeomen of the Guard.

In 1853 his regiment was marching from Peshawur to Kopulvie, and was accompanied by a train of elephants. It was the duty of the mahout in charge of each elephant to prepare twenty chupatties, or flat cakes made of coarse flour, for his charge. When the chupatties were ready, they were placed before the elephant, who, during the process of counting, never attempted to touch one of them until the full number was completed. On the occasion related by Mr. Quay, one of the elephants had seized the opportunity of his mahout's attention being distracted for a moment, to steal and swallow one of the chupatties. When the mahout, having finished the preparation, began to count them out, he of course discovered the theft, and presented his charge with nineteen, in place of the usual number.   The elephant instantly appreciated the fact of their being one less than he had a right to expect, and refused to touch them, expressing his indignation by loud trumpetings.   This brought the conductor of the elephant line (with whom Mr. Quay had been in conversation) on the scene.   Having heard the explanation of the mahout, the conductor decided that the mahout was in fault for not keeping a better look-out, and ordered him to provide the twentieth cake at his own cost.   When this was prepared and added to the pile, the elephant at once accepted and ate them.

It is incredible that an elephant, sagacious as he is, should be able to count up to twenty.   At the same time, it is difficult to find any other explanation, except one which would imply the possession of a still higher degree of intelligence,—namely, the consciousness of his own delinquency, and an expectation (justified by the result) of what would follow when he called the conductor's attention by trumpeting.—I am, Sir, &c.,   ARTHUR CLAY.

March 7, 1891.

THE ELEPHANT'S SAGACITY.

SIR,—Some time ago some interesting stories were told by your correspondents of the display of intelligence by animals. I doubt whether any of these showed greater evidence of reasoning power than was lately exhibited by a young elephant at Belle, the gardens in this city. My son for some weeks visited the gardens daily, sketching the animals, &c. Amongst these is a young "baby" African elephant, decidedly vicious in temper. There are also two or more full-grown elephants. Near their stalls are boxes containing biscuits. When a penny is given to one of the animals, it puts the coin into a slot, and as it falls it releases a biscuit, which the elephant takes with evident satisfaction. Some of the visitors, however, occasionally give the animals a halfpenny, and as experience has taught them that this coin is of no value for the purpose of obtaining biscuits, it is generally thrown contemptuously back to the giver. One day, while my son was present, a visitor gave the "baby" elephant a number of halfpennies in succession, each of which was thrown at him again as soon as received. The visitor then gave the animal two halfpennies at the same time.   His demeanour immediately changed.   For more than five minutes he held the two coins in his trunk, rubbing them together, and now rocking from side to side, and presently seeming to be pondering deeply while perfectly still.   At last he dropped the two halfpence in the box together, with the result that their combined weight gave him the desired biscuit.   The joy of the creature was almost ludicrous.   His big ears were expanded, and he gambolled about in a manner which exhibited the most extravagant delight.   It would seem that he had come to the conclusion that the combined weight of the two coins would produce the desired result.   For, even yet, I believe that he has not learnt to hold one halfpenny in reserve until he gets another.   In other words, he has not learnt to count.   It is only when two are given to him at one time that he appreciates the value of the offering.—I am, Sir, &c.,   GEO. FREEMANTLE.

November 26, 1892.

INFLUENCE OF MUSIC ON ANIMALS.

MUSIC AND ANIMALS.

SIR,—The German tale of a fiddler pursued by wolves alluded to in " Orpheus at the Zoo," in the *Spectator* of October 10th, is the subject of a ballad by Gustav Hartwig, a translation of which, " The Last String," is contained in Sir Theodore Martin's " The Song of the Bell, and other Translations." The fiddler, however, according to the German legend, is not, as recorded in " Orpheus at the Zoo," saved by the accidental breaking of a string, by afterwards playing continuously, but immediately on finding himself surrounded by wolves,—

" He pulls himself up ; in his trembling hand
  The bow across the strings is spanned,
  And they moan, and they groan, and they wail and sing,—
  ' Is there no one, no one, that help will bring ?' "

—I am, Sir, &c., GUSTAV HIRSCH.

October 17, 1891.

MUSIC AND ANIMALS.

SIR,—The extremely interesting articles on "Orpheus at the Zoo," which have lately appeared in the *Spectator*, have suggested to me that possibly you might care for an anecdote which goes to prove that horses can distinguish tunes.

A relation of mine, who has spent many years in India, remembers well how, when living in Lucknow, and enjoying the evening drive, with other English residents in the Indian city, the carriage-horses would toss their heads and paw the ground impatiently when the first notes of "God Save the Queen" were played by the military band every evening. It was the last tune played, the signal for dispersion. A sceptic—or perhaps more than one—having insisted that the horses only knew the tune because it was always played last, and they were able to calculate time, the experiment was tried of playing "God Save the Queen" in the middle, instead of at the end of the evening. Instantly there was the same excitement in the horses standing round "the course," the same impatient tossing of the head and prancing of the feet, the same general stampede and eagerness to start homeward. No one could any longer doubt that they knew and recognised the air ; in fact that they could tell one tune from another.—I am, Sir, &c.,

F. S. H.

October 17, 1891.

MUSIC AND ITS EFFECT ON ANIMALS.

SIR,—To prove that horses can distinguish tunes, let me relate an anecdote given to me by Harley the comedian.   He was walking down the Strand with a brother-actor, who saw in a cab a parti-coloured horse which he thought had belonged to Astley's Circus. They went up to him and patted him, at the same time humming a tune familiar at the Circus.   At once the animal began to dance on his fore-legs, as had been his custom for many years.—I am, Sir, &c.,

B. S.

October 24, 1891.

MUSIC AND ITS INFLUENCE ON ANIMALS.

SIR,—John Wesley once tried the effect of music upon animals, and records the result of his experiment in his " Journals," under date Monday, December 31, 1764 :—" I thought it would be worth while to make an odd experiment. Remembering how surprisingly fond of music the lion at Edinburgh was, I determined to try whether this was the case with all animals of the same kind. I accordingly went to the Tower with one who plays on the German flute. He began playing near four or five lions; only one of these (the rest not seeming to regard it at all) rose up, came to the front of his den, and seemed to be all attention. Meantime a tiger in the same den started up, leaped over the lion's back, turned and ran under his belly, leaped over him again, and so to and fro incessantly. Can we account for this by any principle of mechanism ? Can we account for it at all ? "

There is not, so far as I am aware, any entry in the " Journals " in reference to the Edinburgh lion. Mr. Wesley may, of course, simply have heard or read of this.—I am, Sir, &c., H. J. F.

November 7, 1891.

MISCELLANEOUS STORIES.

ARE ANIMALS MENTALLY HAPPY?

SIR,—Reading Mr. Carlill's article on "Are Animals Mentally Happy?" in this month's *Nineteenth Century*, reminded me of an incident I witnessed in the early summer of 1881 or 1882. Walking one evening in the garden with a friend with whom I was staying in Kent, we heard a great noise amongst the sheep in the park. Fearing a dog was worrying them, we went to see, and saw the sheep collected against the garden wall, and then start off and race, helter-skelter, as fast as they could, to a tree a little distance away ; round it, and then back again—each trying which could be foremost. They then collected, and started off again as before. This they repeated twelve or twenty times, whilst we watched them ; until, seeming tired of their play, they straggled off. This appears to me decidedly a mental act of happiness. The sheep were distinctly at play, and enjoying themselves ; whilst the concerted action, instead of merely singly racing about for physical exercise, showed that their minds were as actively engaged as their bodies.

I can send you the name and address of the lady who witnessed this with me, if you wish for corroboration. She will no doubt remember the circumstance, as she was much amused, and said, " We had no need to go to the races [it was the day of the Derby for that year], because we have had races of our own at home."—I am, Sir, &c., H. R.

June 11, 1887.

A WORD IN DEFENCE OF SHEEP.

SIR,—A writer in the current number of the *Cornhill Magazine* affirms that "there is no stupider animal in all creation" than a sheep; and in a short paper he gives various facts that have come under his notice as a "sheep-herder" in Australia, to support the assertion.

Now, as one whose youth was spent in a sheep district of Scotland, my experience leads to a very different conclusion. In the extensive moors in Dumfriesshire and the South of Lanarkshire, it is quite common for the sheep to pen themselves, leaving the hill-pastures in the evening for some walled field in the low-lying grounds, which they enter by apertures left for them in the "dyke;" and again in the morning they return to the hills, showing remarkable sagacity with respect to the times and everything else connected with their movements. It is a common thing for the cottagers to have pet lambs, which have been given them when the ewes have died, or been too weak to bring up twins. As these pets grow up, nothing could exceed the affection which they manifest for those who tend them, while their intelligence is scarcely inferior to that of a dog.

Every one knows the celebrated picture of "The Pet Lamb," where a butcher's boy is depicted as leading away from the children of a widow their beloved playmate. The wonderful pathos of the picture depends not more on the attachment of the children for the lamb, than on the sagacious animal's reluctance to leave them. The artist who painted that picture —Constable, I think—had not found sheep to be "semi-idiotic."

The eyes of the gazelle have been thought so beautiful, that too often the loveliest human eyes have been likened to them. Now, the eyes of the gazelle and the eyes of some sheep are scarcely distinguishable ; and what the Australian sheep-herder has termed an idiotic and "wild-eyed" look, some close observers have thought to be an expression of infinite tenderness and pathos. The conditions under which the sheep-herder arrived at his conclusions do not seem to me to have been favourable to the true discernment of the animal's nature. "Fiery gallops" among flocks numbering "tens of thousands" are not, I think, the best means of judging the intelligence of a timid animal. There are some intelligent women and men who, if driven by horses at full gallop, and hounded by savage dogs, might behave in an unreasoning manner. If I said tigers or lions instead of dogs, the similitude would be more perfect, as to the sheep a dog is a wolf.

That the Scotch shepherd—an unusually shrewd observer—is of the same opinion as myself regarding his charges, the following anecdote, taken from a

recently published book, will prove. Lord Neaves
was fishing near St. Mary's Loch, and having come
across a shepherd, entered into conversation. The
sheep on the hill-side—through prescience of a coming
storm—were huddled together. on a bare piece of
ground. "If I was one of those sheep," said Lord
Neaves, "I would go where the grass was longer."
"Eh, mon!" was the reply; "but if ye were a sheep,
ye wad hae mair sense."—I am, Sir, &c.,

J. CRAWFORD SCOTT.

December 15, 1888.

HYPNOTISM IN ANIMALS

SIR,—Within the last month I have made an interesting experiment with a fowl. Some choice eggs being
sent me for hatching purposes (having no hen at that
time broody and no incubator) I determined to set
one of my hens on these eggs and keep her there by
the force of mesmeric power. The eggs were not fresh
when I received them, and to keep them with the
uncertain hope of a hen becoming broody might have
been fatal to their hatching, I therefore went against
nature and sat my hen upon these eggs; she was in
full lay at the time, and remained so throughout the
three weeks that she was sitting, laying, according to
her wont, two out of three days. Those who understand poultry will appreciate that no hen will do this,
having become naturally broody, although for the first
day or two after being set on eggs I have had hens lay
once, or even twice. Marking the eggs I set her upon
I was able to know and withdraw the eggs she kept
laying. The first day I placed her on the eggs it took
me half an hour to bring her into a hypnotic condition,
but each successive day, after having roused her to
drink and eat, I was able to soothe her to drowsy

placidity in much less time ; also there were days, for which I can give no reason, when I had to go to her more than once in the day, she being in a restless, excited state, trying to get off the nest. The result has been, much to my own astonishment, that four out of seven of these eggs have hatched, and are healthy, happy little chickens. At night I can still influence their mother to her maternal duties, but in the daytime she takes no notice of them.—I am, Sir, &c.,

E. T. CHAPLIN.

June 7, 1890.

ANIMALS' TOILETTES.

SIR,—In the interesting paper on this subject which appeared in your columns on September 27th, it is well shown that, among other animals, man can claim no monopoly of personal cleanliness; but no allusion is made to one cosmetic operation which is generally supposed to be exclusively human—namely, shaving. It has been discovered that even in this he is not original. There is a pretty South American bird, the Motmot (*Motmotus braziliensis*), which actually begins shaving on arriving at maturity. Naturally adorned with long blue tail-feathers, it is not satisfied with them in their natural state, but with its beak nips off the web on each side for a space of about two inches, leaving a neat little oval tuft at the end of each. Specimens of this bird may be seen at the Natural History Museum at South Kensington, and a full account of it may be found in the Journal of the London Zoological Society for 1873.—I am, Sir, &c.

HERBERT MAXWELL.

October 11, 1890.

THE GUINEA-PIG.

SIR,—I have read with some surprise, in the number of the *Spectator* dated October 18th, the statement that a guinea-pig is incapable of affection. Some years since I had a guinea-pig who would come whenever I called him, who would follow me like a dog even along the streets, and who never seemed happy out of my sight. When I sat down to read, this little creature would come and scratch at my shoes or trousers to coax me to take him up and nurse him. He would sit on his hind legs and hold a book for me to read, and if placed in a corner, would sit in this position for an hour at a time, and seemed to delight in it. After having him several years, I was seized with a severe attack of congestion of the lungs, which confined me to my bed for upwards of a month ; just as I was getting over this, my friends told me that my guinea-pig had been ill for some time, and that he refused to eat anything, but that they did not like to mention it to me before. I at once had him brought to me ; he was miserably thin, and could scarcely walk, but he at once took food from my hands,

no matter what I offered him.   After some little time, scarcely an hour, I think, he gave two or three little gasps, turned over on his side, and died in my lap.— .
I am, Sir, &c.,   JOHN BROWNING.

November 8, 1890.

MUSIC AND ANIMALS.

SIR,—I venture to give expression to a hope that your "Orpheus" will make public some more results of his interesting musical experiments upon the inhabitants of the Zoo. His recent articles in the *Spectator* open up the important subject of the varying musical tastes possessed by different men and beasts. Dr. Seemann, quoted by Darwin, states that " by travelling eastwards we find that there is certainly a different language of music. Songs of joy and dance-accompaniments are no longer, as with us, in the major keys, but always in the minor." Nor will it be denied, I think, that even in Western Europe, as late as the sixteenth century, minor keys were far more prevalent in joyful music, such as carols and dances, than they are at the present day. I know of several musical people who show a decided preference for minor over major. Is this a case of reversion to an earlier type? "Orpheus" could throw important light on the relative efficacy of the two modes with musical beasts—such, for instance, as seals are if hunters speak truly.

It is also most desirable that the effects of brass, wood, wind, and instruments of percussion should be systematically tried in the Zoo; and perhaps some enterprising exhibitor of savage musicians will some day carry these experiments still further. Only by these means shall we discover whether the notions of beauty in music undoubtedly possessed by many beasts are more nearly allied to those of civilised or of barbarous nations.—I am, Sir, &c.,

E. C. MARCHANT.

October 17, 1891.

A TAME HARE.

SIR,—In your interesting article on "Possible Pets," in the *Spectator* of January 2nd, I see you ask : Who, since the days of Cowper, has seen a tame hare? Will you allow me to tell you of one in a country-house in the West of Ireland, whose acquaintance I made last summer? The little creature was brought in by the mowers during hay-harvest, very young, very frightened, and wounded. A scythe had accidentally cut off one of his ears as he lay hidden in the long grass. By the time the wound was healed he had become tame, and when I saw him he was quite at home in his new surroundings as an indoor pet. He was most caressing and affectionate, and would nestle in your arms, or climb up and sit on your shoulder. He had the run of the large drawing-room, a tiny ball of brown fur, with one long ear and a pair of bright eyes. He ran noiselessly about over carpets and rugs, and in the dusk of the late summer evenings it was often difficult to find him. The Irish terrier, however, never failed to do so. My hostess would say, "'Judy,' find 'Coco,'" and in a few minutes the truant's hiding-place was discovered. "Judy' never hurt him, and he never seemed afraid of the dog. My hostess allowed him to run about on the lawn, at first with many fears lest he should escape and desert his friends, but "Coco" never seemed in the least anxious to do so; he would run on a few steps in front of her and stop to nibble the grass, and allow her to catch him again as soon as she thought he had had enough air and exercise. He was too young to judge of his intelligence, but even in his babyhood he was a delightful pet, and I have no doubt by this time he is a hare of many accomplishments, as three months ago he was "the hare with many friends."—I am, Sir, &c., M. F. B.

January 23, 1892.

A TAME HARE.

SIR,—You may possibly be interested in knowing that a tame hare is a constant drawing-room companion of certain friends of mine who are living near here (London, W.).

At tea-time "Monk" is entertained with bread-and-milk, but his usual food consists of oats, and he has a special delight in dandelions. His playfellow is a large collie-dog, who is frequently reminded by some sharp "taps" of the paw, that the "manners" of the drawing-room are not to be those of the field. His musical sense seems wonderfully developed ; for with the pianoforte-playing of some he seems pleased, while with that of others he always shows himself, in scampering about the room, quite the reverse.—I am, Sir, &c.,   S.

February 6, 1892.

HUMOROUS APES.

SIR,—If you care to have your good stories of the humour of animals capped, here are two or three more. I remember, in a description of India or Ceylon some forty years ago, a story of an Englishman who had a monkey. Looking out of his window one day, he saw his cook getting a fowl ready for boiling, while the monkey lay on the ground shamming death, and a party of crows stood at a little distance, divided between the desire for the kitchen offal, and the fear of the possibly shamming monkey. One crow, more adventurous than the rest, came within the magic distance, and was instantly in the clutch of the monkey. At the same moment, the cook, having finished trussing the fowl, put it into the pot and went away. The monkey plucked his crow as he had just seen the cook pluck the fowl, took the fowl out of the pot, put the crow in, and retired with his exchange. When the cook came back, and saw the fowl left preparing for his master's luncheon turned black, he was, as may be supposed, struck mad with terror at this manifest intervention of the Evil One.

Another story, some forty or fifty years earlier, is

of a monkey which my uncle brought to London from India.   On one occasion he was seen playing with the ink, perhaps writing a letter, in his master's bed-room.   He upset the ink, and thereupon he went to the chest of drawers, opened a drawer, took out a shirt, and wiped up the ink with it.   On another day he was sitting in my grandmother's drawing-room (it was in Hill Street), when another lady came in and sat down.   The monkey, after watching her for some time from the back of the chair on which he was perched, snatched the visitor's bonnet from her head, put it on his own, and defied all attempts to catch him and rescue the bonnet.   At last, the window being open, he leapt out upon the lamp-post, and there sat, sharing the delight of the passers-by, looking as Blucher must have looked when, years after, he appeared on the field of Waterloo in an old lady's bonnet.

In these instances the love of mischievous, prac-tical joking is manifest : it is probable, if not so cer-tain, in a story of an eminent naturalist (I forget his name) who was hoping to develop the intelligence of a monkey to whose education he was devoting him-self.   One day he saw with delight that the monkey was sitting at the other end of the room, turning over the leaves of a valuable book on entomology and looking at the plates with apparent interest.   But on going nearer, he saw, with dismay, that the monkey was turning over the plates in order that, when he came to a particularly large beetle or butterfly, he might pick it out and eat it.   As the paper could not have had a nice taste, I think he may have been actuated rather by the fun of the thing than by a mere depraved appetite. Perhaps he was verifying the like method of learning among the philosophers of Laputa. But this I leave to the judicious consideration of yourself and your readers.—I am, Sir, &c., E. S.

October 8, 1892.

THE BEAVERS AT THE ZOO.

SIR,—In your review of the book on beavers, in the *Spectator* of January 28th, I think you are unfairly severe on the want of intelligence in the performances of the beavers at the Zoo. Perhaps your reviewer has never had to do his work in a building with a corrugated iron roof. My work is done under that mean and ineffectual substitute for thatch, and summer suns and winter frosts make one feel the beavers' great wisdom in recognising the insufficiency of the covering provided for them.

Had I a suitable supply of mud, and had I a flat tail, together with that so seldom-achieved though so often-desired "combination of industry and leisure," I too would strive after greater perfection in building, and my roof too would then be, like the savages, "neatly though inexpensively clothed in mud."—I am, Sir, &c., H. S.

February 11, 1893.

THE SAGACITY OF BEARS.

SIR,—I was interested to observe in the ¡Zoological Gardens at Hanley this summer the faculty which bears possess of putting two and two together. If a biscuit is thrown into the bath in their den, they will, in order to avoid getting wet, go round to the further side of the bath and paddle with their feet in the water till they have caused the biscuit to float across the bath to the edge where it can easily be reached by them. One wonders how they first learnt this.—I am, Sir, &c., C. W. H. KENRICK.

November 9, 1895.

ANIMAL STORIES.

SIR,—Having read in your paper many curious stories illustrating the instincts of dogs and cats, it seems to me that the following, relating to sheep and ducks, may prove interesting. Many years ago I had a conversation with Mr. Hassall, who was the first settler in King George's Sound, on the difficulties he encountered in establishing a flock of sheep there. He started operations, assisted only by convicts who acted as shepherds. He told me that many of his imported sheep died from eating poisonous herbs or shrubs, but this was not the case with native-born animals, and that he did not know of a single death from poison of any sheep bred in the country.—I am, Sir, &c.,   W. H. CHALLIS.

November 30, 1895.

THE SAGACITY OF BEARS.

SIR,—Referring to your correspondent's letter, in the *Spectator* of November 9th, noticing the faculty which bears possess of putting two and two together, I wonder whether any of your readers have observed the same thing with regard to some of the elephants in the Zoological Gardens in London. For when a child, in throwing a biscuit to the elephant, dropped it between the cage and the barrier, and out of reach of the child or the elephant, the latter blew the biscuit with its trunk till the child could reach it, and again attempt to throw it into the elephant's mouth. This happened not once, but several times. Not that elephants have perfect reasoning powers, as the sequel to this story will show. After the small child had made many vain attempts to throw the biscuit far enough, a good-natured lad standing near thought he would help, so he took the biscuit from the child. This displeased the elephant, who thereupon dealt the lad a severe blow on the arm, causing him a good deal of pain.—I am, Sir, &c., A. MOSSOP.

November 30, 1895.

RECENT RAT-LORE.

SIR,—In your article in the *Spectator* of November
9th, under the above heading, you remark that rats
transporting eggs on level ground, were observed by
Mr. Battye to roll them "in front of them with their
chests." A deceased acquaintance of mine, who had
a tame white rat, told me that he once saw it carrying
off an egg in the following fashion. The egg was
supported underneath by a front paw, being pierced
and steadied by the upper incisors, and was thus
carried safely forward by the rat on its three dis-
engaged feet.—I am, Sir, &c., H. J. BUSHBY.

November 30, 1895.

RATS.

SIR,—*A propos* of your interesting article on "Recent Rat-lore," in the *Spectator* of November 9th, the incidents named from Mr. H. C. Barkley's graphic "Studies on Rat-catching," suggest my writing to narrate a clever exploit of a retriever dog belonging to the housekeeper of a well-known newspaper office in the Strand. Rats are constantly caught on the premises, and the dog, fully aware of their habits, evinces such ability that his intelligence is quite worthy of record. Last Sunday he was heard barking loudly, calling for assistance, in the compositors' room, where there is a rat-hole in the floor. The dog had watched two fine rats come up through their hole, and immediately they were fairly away from their point of entry he rushed up and sat on the hole to cut off their means of retreat, barking forthwith for help. Nothing would induce him to budge till a board was brought and placed over the hole, when he started in pursuit, and soon despatched the intruders. His master assures me that the dog originated this ingenious method of procedure, and that he has practised it with like success on several other occasions.—I am, Sir, &c., MAURICE B. ADAMS.

November, 30, 1895.

INDEX.

www.ingramcontent.com/pod-product-compliance
Lightning Source LLC
Chambersburg PA
CBHW021038030726
47496CB00006B/1597